The Parnas

The shaded part of the map shows the section of Pisa south of the Arno River, which was occupied by the American troops on August 1, 1944. The light part of the map indicates the area north of the Arno, occupied by the Germans.

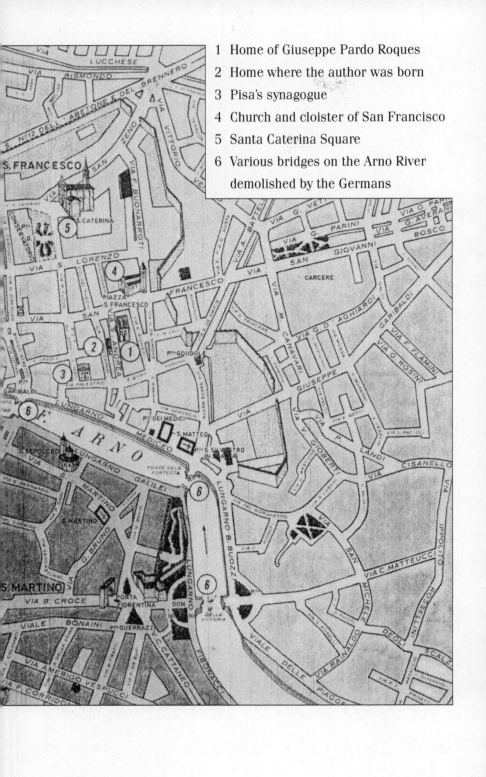

1 Home of Giuseppe Pardo Roques
2 Home where the author was born
3 Pisa's synagogue
4 Church and cloister of San Francisco
5 Santa Caterina Square
6 Various bridges on the Arno River
demolished by the Germans

ALSO BY SILVANO ARIETI

American Handbook of Psychiatry (Editor-in-Chief)

Interpretation of Schizophrenia
(National Book Award for Science)

The Will to Be Human

Creativity: The Magic Synthesis

Understanding and Helping the Schizophrenic

Abraham and the Contemporary Mind

The Parnas

A Scene from the Holocaust

Silvano Arieti

Foreword by Harold S. Kushner

PAUL DRY BOOKS

Philadelphia 2000

First Paul Dry Books Edition, 2000

Paul Dry Books, Inc., Philadelphia, Pennsylvania
www.pauldrybooks.com

Copyright © 1979 Paul Dry Books, Inc.
Foreword copyright © 1981 Harold S. Kushner
Text type: Adobe Garamond
Display type: Fenice Family
Composed by Duke & Company
Designed by Adrianne Onderdonk Dudden

Printed in the United States of America

Library of Congress Cataloging-in-Publication Data

Arieti, Silvano.
    The parnas : a scene from the Holocaust / Silvano Arieti ;
foreword by Harold S. Kushner. — 1st Paul Dry Books ed.
        p. cm.
    Previously published: New York : Basic Books, c1979.
    ISBN 0-9664913-0-0 (pbk.)
    1. Pardo Roques, Giuseppe.   2. Jews—Italy—Pisa Biography.
3. Holocaust, Jewish (1939–1945)—Italy—Pisa.   4. Pisa (Italy)—
Ethnic relations.   I. Title.
DS135. I85P5729 1999
940.53'18'092—dc21
    [B]   99-41323
                                                        CIP

ISBN 978-0-9664913-0-2

To Yolanda and Giampaolo Rocca

Contents

Foreword

by Harold S. Kushner

The number Six Million overwhelms the mind. Our imaginations are too limited to comprehend so many individual men, women and children, victims of the Holocaust. After the first dozen or two, they tend to blur, to become nameless, faceless statistics. Only when the uniqueness of one of the victims can be captured does the Holocaust take on a human, rather than a statistical, character. Anne Frank is the best-known example of that process. Giuseppe Pardo Roques, parnas of the Jewish community of Pisa, Italy, is another.

This book should be better known to Jewish readers and students of the fields of mental health. When a man as distinguished as Silvano Arieti writes about the Holocaust, he deserves our attention. In this brief, deceptively simple narrative, Arieti has told the story of Giuseppe Pardo, parnas (lay leader) of his native community of Pisa, and of his death at the hands of the Nazis. Pardo was the leading citizen of a small Jewish community that produced more than its share of distinguished Jews. He was a learned man, familiar with Bible, Talmud, and secular subjects. He was a wealthy man, and charitable to Jew and non-Jew alike. (He ultimately met his death together with six fellow Jews and five gentiles who had sought the protection of his home.) And he was a profoundly neurotic man, who had an irrational fear of animals, especially dogs. When he walked in the streets of Pisa—which was not often because of his fears—he would swing a cane from side to side behind him to drive away the imaginary animals.

Because of those fears, Pardo, a man of means, never traveled. When the war came, he remained in his home in Pisa, relying on the good will of the Italian authorities to protect him. By the summer of 1944, however, Italy had surrendered, and German soldiers were occupying its northern regions. In August, Nazi soldiers broke into the Pardo home and murdered the parnas and his houseguests. The wild animals he feared had in fact caught up with him.

Arieti, however, has done more than simply tell the story of a man who deserves to be redeemed from anonymity. As a psychiatrist, he has used the confrontation of Giuseppe Pardo and the Nazis to tell us something about the human soul, how allegedly rational people can be cruel and unfeeling, and how "mentally ill" people can be immensely compassionate and even heroic, not despite but as a dimension of their neuroses.

There are millions of unique stories that could be told about victims of the Holocaust, and we are enriched to have this one told with such sensitivity and insight.

The Parnas

Only gleanings shall be left,
As when an olive tree is beaten:
Two berries or three on the topmost branch,
Four or five on the many-branched bough.   ISAIAH 17:6

I will fear no evil,
for Thou art with me.   PSALM 23

Introduction

Since the title of this book may strike readers as unfamiliar, they may have no inkling of what the book is about. To begin with, I must make it clear that most of what I am going to report is fact. I have known the main character of the story since my childhood. The other characters in the book—the guests, the servants, the neighbors, and the strange visitors on that eventful summer day —were people who really existed. The names by which they are identified are their real names. Only one character has been added: a young man I have named Angelo Luzzatto. He is a composite of several people, all real, and all known to the community I describe.

The events I am about to recount took place in my hometown, Pisa. When I returned there after an absence of many years, I interviewed witnesses to the events of my story, questioned people to verify what I had heard, and ascertained the truth of most of the things that I am going to report. When the people in my story speak, I have had to put into their mouths the words I thought they would be likely to say. In the case of the main character, whom I knew so well, this was easy. And in the thirty years and more since I first heard the facts, began to collect the details, and meditated over the meaning, these words have always been with me. Time and time again they have echoed through my mind.

This is a story of suffering and fear, but it is also more. It is the account of a discovery I made by means of that suffering, one that has deeply affected my life and my work. I have been a psychiatrist for many years, and the discovery concerns the nobility and greatness that are at times hidden within mental illness. Yes, I have come to believe that mental illness may hide and express the spirituality of man. It is my wish here to acquaint readers with my discovery by introducing them to the man who was called "the parnas."

Central to my story is another illness, the epidemic of evil that seized Europe in the 1930s and 1940s and was the most ferocious of its kind ever to appear on earth. Since this illness swept over the Western world in our lifetime, it is incumbent upon us to expose it in the most minute detail. Each of us who survived has the obligation to reveal what he came to know. Sometimes one moment, fully understood, can shed light on the whole.

But I hope this book will show something else: that strange bond which at times links the nobility of the first and personal illness to the perversity of the second and social one. I hope the reader will join the main character of the story, and its author, in the search for this mysterious connection.

I have asked myself why I waited so long before writing this story. Why did I let long stretches of time pass during which I refused to think about this subject, so that several times I had to reattune myself to a story I knew so well? Whatever the answer, each time my mind and heart went back to the episodes narrated in this book, I saw new possibilities for meaning, and the hope was renewed that the day would come when I could share my understanding with others. That day has now come. It is now my duty to tell the story as I have come to see it. It is my sacred duty to do what I can so that the story and its characters will be remembered, and so that its meaning can be pondered.

I feel as if I had written this book not only with ink but also with blood. On page after page I could not evade the claims being made on my soul. It was not easy to return this way to a time that I might have been caught in but avoided, and that I now have to live over and over again. It was not easy to collect tears that I neither shed nor saw in others but that still burn in my eyes.

I hope this short book will also show that tragic times have a perfume of their own, and smiles of hope, and traces of charm, and offer olive branches and late warnings that may not be too late.

A Special Community

I have lived in New York City for several decades, but my hometown is Pisa, the birthplace of Galileo and, of course, the city of the leaning tower. To escape the Fascists I left Pisa in the early part of January 1939, at the age of twenty-four, and came to live in the United States. Shortly before I left, I was graduated from the medical school of Pisa, intending to become a psychiatrist. I owe it to my Aunt Yolanda that I was able to leave Italy and come to the United States—an event that both saved my life and gave it a special direction. Yolanda discovered that in Switzerland we could get American visas in a hurry. She went to Montreux and then to Zurich, making all the necessary contacts and inquiries. My brother and I were to go to Switzerland on separate days, on the pretext of going skiing, and from there make our way to America. The plan had to be carried out secretly. Yolanda, only nine years older than I, together with my uncle Giampaolo, who accompanied me to junior high school the first day classes were held, are the persons to whom this book is dedicated.

My last few days in Pisa were spent mostly with my parents. They were as determined to remain in Italy as they were eager for my brother and me to leave.

I also said goodbye to two or three people who were very important to me. One of these was Giuseppe Pardo Roques, the *parnas*. This Hebrew word, pronounced with the accent on the second syllable, is commonly used by Sephardic Jews and means "leader," generally the president of the congregation. I remember hearing the word for the first time in the synagogue when I was a child. My grandfather, Giacomo Bemporad, pointed to Giuseppe Pardo Roques and whispered, "That's the parnas." My grandfather did not have the patience to explain what "parnas" meant, but noticing the deferential way people acted toward this very dignified man, I grasped the meaning of the word. I realized that, together with the rabbi, Pardo was the person holding the highest position in the synagogue. He used to sit in his own special seat in a section to the right of the altar that was reserved for prominent persons. I can still remember the seating arrangement in this section of the synagogue. Next to the altar was the seat of Rabbi Augusto Hasdà; then came the seat of Cantor Salomone Cassuto; then the most prominent member of our congregation, David Supino, who had been made a lifetime senator of the kingdom of Italy. And next to David Supino sat the parnas. These persons were the only ones in the congregation to have chairs with *braccioli* (that is, arms).

So, in early January 1939, I went to see the parnas. He received me, as he had done so many times before, in his spacious living room. I told him that I was about to leave Italy, and that I had come to say goodbye. I said I hoped that both he and my parents would also decide to leave. We were sitting facing each other. He spoke to me firmly but gently; he was sixty-four years old and I twenty-four, but the forty years' difference in our ages was dissolved by his tender way of making me feel accepted and the object of his concern.

He said, "Thank you for coming to see me, Silvano. I agree that the best thing for you is to go. I am sorry to see you leave. I have known you since you were born. Please, write to me. I understand your hope that your parents and I will leave Italy, but each of us has to do what he believes right and appropriate. Each of us has to be true to himself and to what he seeks from life. I believe I must stay here; your parents have to decide for themselves. As for you, I know you have made the right choice. You will do well in America, Silvano. I have confidence in you. Perhaps one day you will come back to Pisa and visit me. You will be full of knowledge and wisdom, and you will be able to help me."

I was not sure what he meant. I knew that, for him, to be true to what one seeks from life meant to be true to one's calling; but what did he mean when he said that perhaps I would be able to help him? Certainly not with the administration of the congregation. Did he mean help in a personal way? Had he discovered my secret? Had he figured out that I intended to become a psychiatrist because of him, because the strange illness that afflicted him had always stirred my imagination and had played a major part in my ambition to be of help to others? I did not ask him then. I was moved and felt too respectful to question him. I do not remember how I answered. Our meeting was short. In the past, sometimes he spoke tersely, sometimes he was rather verbose. That time he was brief. We shook hands and parted.

Who was this Giuseppe Pardo Roques (whom I shall refer to as Signor Pardo, Pardo, or Giuseppe)? As parnas, one of his main occupations was to see to the continuity of both the religious and the philanthropic services of the congregation. This was not an easy task, for the Jewish congregation of Pisa had undergone a steady decline in the twentieth century—especially as more and more of its members had moved to larger cities. Thus there had been a sharp decrease in available funds. But money was not the most urgent problem. Pardo himself was a very wealthy man. As a bachelor with no family to provide for, he might easily have felt that there was no better way to use his money than by turning to black the red figures in the account books of the congregation. The real difficulty was the scarcity of people willing to share the various obligations that kept the congregation going. Pardo spent most of his time in administration, including looking after the elementary school associated with the synagogue, where I myself had learned to read and write. I remember very well how he used to come to inspect the school. He was very much interested in me and in my progress; I had no doubt that he had faith in me. He once gave me a children's book about the Old Testament, which I still have. Nothing pleased me more than to hear him and my teacher praise my "brilliance." This made me happy, but it also provoked some apprehension in me lest I not live up to their expectations.

Pardo did not limit his charitable activities to the Jewish community but was a real "benefactor"—as he was usually called—of Christian and nondenominational groups as well. Friday was the day of the poor people at Pardo's house. People in trouble—those who had no money for medicines or doctors, for instance, or no means to buy a railroad ticket to visit a sick child in a different city, or, more frequently, literally no money for a decent lunch or supper—could knock at Pardo's door on Friday, certain of being received, heard, helped. Pardo also distributed tokens that could be exchanged for meals at a restaurant in the square of the food market, where he had made special arrangements. His beneficiaries had only to state their case, which was accepted on faith. No identity papers were needed. Over 99 percent of the people who came on Friday were Christians. Pardo's only request was that they come before sunset, when the Sabbath starts.

The Pardo family had lived for many generations in a sumptuous home in Sant' Andrea Street, a street where many Jews as well as many Christians lived. Pardo's house was opposite the house of my grandparents, where I was born. Its address was number 22, and my grandparents' was number 23. Even today, there are a few old people who remember when the Pardo family had a horse, a fiacre, and a coachman in uniform. Later the horse and the French-style coach were replaced by a car and a chauffeur.

Pardo's home must have had about twenty-five rooms—I never counted them—and a beautiful garden. In the garden there was a well that always provided drinking water, even during those occasional hot summers when there was a drought. Near the well was a fountain, whose running water was provided by the well.

The room that I knew best in his house was the one in which he received me when I went to say goodbye to him. It was on the main floor, and from it we could see the garden. It was beautifully furnished, with no ostentation but with many valuable objects, books, and paintings that revealed the highest of both Italian and Hebrew culture. For at least two decades this room had been a cultural salon.

I was in that salon several times between 1932 and 1938. During most of that period, or at least between 1932 and 1937, Mussolini had not yet become anti-Semitic or pro-Nazi. As a matter of fact, in 1934, when Hitler organized the assassination of the Austrian Chancellor Dollfuss in order to prepare for the *Anschluss* (the union of Austria to Germany), Mussolini sent two divisions to the Brenner Pass and committed himself to defending the independence of Austria. Moreover, in April 1935 Italy had participated in the Conference of Stresa and signed an agreement condemning the violations perpetrated by Nazi Germany and reaffirming the spirit of the Treaty of Locarno. It was after the Ethiopian War (1935–1936) that Mussolini became tied to Hitler and engaged more and more in the latter's anti-Semitic program. While out-and-out alliance with the Nazis was to wait until the late 1930s, Fascism had exercised a chilling influence over the whole of Italian culture from the beginning of the Mussolini dictatorship in 1925.

In Pisa the Fascists brought about a drastic restriction of the famous local university. Under these circumstances Pardo's salon became the place where people of all ages, including young people like me, could meet well-known professors or celebrities who had come from many lands to lecture at the university or to visit Pardo.

In his home we felt we could breathe clean air. Pardo himself was an eloquent speaker despite an odd nasal timbre to his voice. I used to admire his style. He was equally at ease with the most erudite language and the simplest popular expressions; sometimes his sentences were formal classic structures, sometimes pieces of common Tuscan dialogue. When he spoke, there was a quality in Pardo that is difficult to define. All of us agreed that his extraordinary lucidity made him almost irresistibly persuasive. Yet this quality I speak of—call it hypnotic—frequently overtook people even before he could set out his persuasive arguments.

It was in Pardo's salon that I first heard discussions of Martin Buber and existentialism. It was there that I first heard of Ahad Haam, the great Zionist thinker. It was there that I first heard Freud and psychoanalysis being talked about openly—especially by an authority on the subject, Professor Enzo Bonaventura.

I cannot here name all the people I met in Pardo's salon, but one man particularly—Nahum Sokolow—stands out vividly in my memory. Sokolow was at that time president of the World Zionist Organization, the successor to Chaim Weizmann. As a writer, Sokolow has been credited with introducing a new style to Hebrew literature, a blending of Western secularism and religious mysticism. When we heard him (I cannot recollect the exact date, but I believe it must have been in 1934, when I was twenty) Sokolow, now an old man, spoke with a mixture of anxiety and hope about the hard times ahead for the Zionist cause. The Nazis had come to power in Germany, and the United States—which was Zionism's main source of financial support—was going through a severe economic depression.

Pardo himself was versed not only in biblical and talmudic studies but also in modern literature, philosophy, and all the political currents and movements that brought so much upheaval to Europe in the first four decades of the twentieth century. The horizons of provincial life, restricted by Fascist nationalism, in Pardo's home were made to open out on the great world. It was there in that salon, with its very special blend of Hebrew intellectuality and passionate internationalism, that I was given my first preparation for what was to become my American life. Pardo's salon was an outpost of my hometown-to-be, New York City.

But all this only begins my story of the parnas of Pisa. In addition to his authority, wisdom, beneficence, and wide culture, I must mention that Giuseppe Pardo Roques was mentally ill. Indeed his illness, recognized and overlooked by all, is of great significance to this story. And even though I am a psychiatrist, I must stress that its importance is not that of a case history.

What exactly Pardo's mental illness was, might be a matter of psychiatric debate. Its most obvious symptoms were phobias, that is, fears that have no justification. Most of all, Pardo was afraid of animals—mice, rats, cats, and especially dogs. I remember seeing him pass by on his daily walk. He always carried a cane, which he frequently switched behind his back from one hand to the other with a semicircular motion. He was using the cane to explore and to reassure himself that no dogs or other animals were around. He used the cane in the way blind people do, except that instead of exploring what was ahead of him, he explored what was in back of him and could not be seen. Although he followed this procedure slowly and with great discretion, the purpose of what he was doing was obvious to those who had become accustomed to seeing him. Some pitied him, some laughed at him.

In any case, a mountain of rumors had come to center on his peculiar habits. One would often hear someone talking about Pardo's ridiculous gestures or laughing about the way he labored to avoid what was not there. It was said that when he thought he was alone, he would repeat elaborate rituals for hours and hours, each ritual designed to reassure him that there were no animals nearby. He had to choose between the agonizing rituals or the terror of an attack of panic. On certain days these phobias would follow him like ghosts no matter where he went. On other days when he experienced intense fears everywhere, Pardo would be forced to stay home in his bedroom or study.

And yet, when he appeared in administrative capacities, at public functions, at social gatherings, in public debates, or at the Ravvivati, Pisa's most aristocratic club, he displayed the most gentle and dignified bearing. Moreover, he showed himself to be an utterly fearless man, courageously prepared to defend the underprivileged, the underdog, the distressed in any way—in short, anyone beset by a realistic fear and confronted with a realistic danger. Thus his almost constant fear was accompanied by a constantly available courage. The continuous pattern of seeing danger to himself for which no help was available was companion to a pattern of promptly providing help for the suffering of fearful others. But other people's fears and dangers were recognized by the world; his own fears, in their fully tragic intensity, were known only to himself.

Some of the young boys of the town openly made fun of Pardo or played tricks on him. On Saturday morning Italian boys go to school, but occasionally a Saturday would be a school holiday. It was especially on these days that the boys were sure to catch Pardo when he left the synagogue after the morning service. Now and then they would hide with a dog at a corner of the street where he used to turn and push the animal toward him. At other times they would imitate the barking of a dog. Pardo tried his best to overcome panic, and he often succeeded. He acted as if he did not hear or see; he changed routes and tried his best to maintain the dignity that his age and position required. Even the students of the University of Pisa, who by age and education should have known better, would sometimes publish unsavory vignettes about him that were supposed to be funny. On the whole, though, the population of Pisa respected him. The people in his neighborhood liked him, and the poor loved him. He was the learned man, the benefactor, the only man in Pisa always ready to extend a hand to both Christians and Jews.

The fears that I have mentioned, and probably others, very largely restricted Pardo's life. He could not go far away from his home because he was afraid he would be exposed to the sight of animals. Thus he never traveled. With the tactlessness of a teenager I once asked him why he never went on vacations or visited places dear to him, like Jerusalem. He hesitated before answering, then said, "My health does not permit me to travel." He did not go further, but it was obvious that by health he meant mental health. Since I admired the man, in my private thoughts I compared him to the great philosopher Immanuel Kant, who in his long life never once traveled outside his native Koenigsberg. Great minds receive inspiration from an inner source, an inner life, I said to myself, and did not need the stimuli of new and different environments.

I believe now that Pardo's condition might have been more severe than a simple phobic one. It occurs to me that in some periods of great anxiety he might even have had quasi-hallucinatory experiences, that is, the impression of seeing or hearing the dreaded animals.

My father, who was a physician, had been Pardo's doctor for several years. My father, however, was a general practitioner. Although he must have known a good deal about the symptoms of Signor Pardo, he maintained the strictest professional confidentiality and never told us a word about him. My guess is that Signor Pardo must have consulted a few psychiatrists but soon gave up because none of them had been able to help him in any way.

I was very much taken up with his problem. As I have already mentioned, I attribute my main motivation for pursuing psychiatric studies to my relationship with Pardo. His illness had an aura of mystery that I hoped I could unveil one day. No matter how bizarre his behavior could be or how it verged on the ridiculous, to me it seemed insignificant compared to the inner turmoil from which it so clearly derived. How powerful that inner turbulence must be, I thought, if its visible manifestations could not be held in check by even so powerful a mind and character. I wished he could be helped, maybe by me one day; yes, by me. Thus when he said that perhaps on my return I could be of help to him, I felt a pang of pain at having been discovered, at having possibly revealed my presumptuousness, and yet at the same time I felt reaffirmed in my secret wish.

I was inclined to think that there were psychological reasons for Pardo's condition; but these reasons, of course, could not be traced without subjecting him to prolonged psychoanalytic therapy. And there was nobody capable of doing that type of work. What I could do at that time—and what I did do—was defend him from people's cruel tongues. When I heard insinuations about the reason Pardo had remained a bachelor, I strongly asserted my conviction that he was a bachelor because he did not want to impose the crippling restrictions of his illness on a wife. From the way in which he occasionally joked or spoke about women, I knew that he was not at all oblivious to the opposite sex.

But not only was Pardo's illness crucial in my having decided to become a psychiatrist in the first place; I also feel that it determined my attitude toward the mental patient in general, an attitude that was to become a major asset in my therapeutic efforts. I learned from Pardo's situation to see the mentally ill patient not simply as somebody to cure or to pity—that is, as someone whose assertions are not to be taken quite seriously—but as a person who, in addition to his illness, or in spite of his illness, or because of his illness, may have profound insight or wisdom to offer. This attitude, first learned from my acquaintance with the parnas, has only intensified with the passage of time, when I have been able to reflect on how much I have learned from mental patients, not just about illness, but about life itself.

Nevertheless, an important question arises about the Jews of Pisa: How could they have selected so ill a man to be their elder? Granted that he exercised the functions of parnas well, the fact remains that his handicaps were known to the whole city. Some people, as I have said, made fun of them. Beyond that, there was always the danger that at some time or other the chief of the congregation would go into a state of panic not compatible with the dignity of his position. Was his acceptance due to the money he poured into the dwindling funds of the congregation?

The answer, I believe, is that the admiration in which the community held him far outweighed any doubts raised by the spectacle of his illness. My impression is that the Pisan Jews regarded one's mental illness as a matter of private concern, unless it was dangerous to others. Now, at just what point a mental illness is to be viewed as tolerable or as intolerable, or at what point it should prevent a person from holding public office, is hard to say. These limits have never been defined, and down to today they remain a subject of public discussion among psychiatrists, politicians, patients, and former patients. In the case of Pardo, I hope that the unfolding of this story will shed some light on the question.

First, then, it might be worthwhile to turn our attention to the Pisan Jewish community, the people who time after time would unanimously vote Pardo into the position of parnas.

At the time I left Italy, there were 280 Jews in Pisa; a small group but noticeable. Among them were a few university professors, a senator, doctors, lawyers, keepers of small or middle-sized stores, a family of industrialists, a blind beggar, a homosexual who taught mathematics and openly disclosed his sexual orientation, a few peddlers, and some blue-collar workers. Fundamentally conservative in the way they lived, they were in the avantgarde in the realm of attitudes and ideas. Though they stood together as a group, each one of them was a strong individualist, and a rather opinionated one. As much as they differed in economic status, social prestige, and education, most of them felt very close to one another. This closeness did not prevent them from having basically different ideas, even with respect to Jewish affairs and such things as the way Jews should feel about the Mussolini government. There were some who, together with the rabbi, Augusto Hasdà, considered themselves to be Italians of the Jewish religion without any allegiance to the international Jewish organizations that were sponsoring a return of Jews to the land of Israel.

In Turin such Jews, Jewish by religion only, published a periodical called *Our Flag* (*La Nostra Bandiera*). The majority of Italian Jews, who favored Zionism, nicknamed this paper *Our Fear* (*La Nostra Paura*), in the belief that only fear of irritating the nationalist government was inducing this kind of Jew to be a public anti-Zionist. But whatever the motive of many *Our Flag* Jews, some, like our rabbi, were sincerely fundamentalist in their Judaism. They believed that a return to the land of Israel should occur only by divine, not political, intervention. Most Pisan Jews, however, including Pardo, were in favor of a Jewish homeland in the biblical land of Israel.

Although it was always very small, the Jewish congregation of Pisa has an old and venerable history. Jews were living in the city long before the famous leaning tower was built. Benjamin of Tudela, a Jew born in Spain in the kingdom of Navarre, went on a long journey between 1159 and 1167 from his native Spain to Persia for the purpose of visiting and describing all the Jewish communities that he could find. He visited the south of France, Italy, Greece, Constantinople, Syria, Palestine, Persia, Yemen, Egypt, western Germany, and the north of France, and then he went back to Spain, where he wrote his famous book *The Travels of Benjamin*.

The first Italian city that Benjamin mentions is Genoa, where he found only two Jewish families. From Genoa Benjamin went on to Pisa, a journey that at that time required two days of traveling. In Pisa he found not fewer than twenty Jewish families. It is impossible to guess how many of the Pisan Jews that Benjamin encountered, if any, were descendants of those Jews who had been granted legal residence in lands ruled by Rome when Julius Caesar made Judaism a legal religion and granted definite privileges and exemptions to its adherents. Perhaps some were descendants of the prisoners that the Emperor Titus brought to Italy after destroying the Second Temple. Perhaps some had recently arrived in Pisa, then a flourishing maritime republic that maintained a very active Levantine trade.

The little trading community that Benjamin of Tudela found in Pisa continued to exist throughout the subsequent centuries and still exists today. In the thirteenth and the beginning of the fourteenth centuries, Jews who resided in Tuscany were referred to as Pisan citizens. During the Spanish Inquisition, which required Jews residing in Spain to make one of three choices—convert to Christianity, burn at the stake, or leave Spain—many took refuge in other countries, and some went to Italy, bringing with them their Sephardic culture. *Sephardic,* in the Hebrew etymology, means "Spanish"; but as the word has come to be used, it refers to all the Jews who themselves once lived or whose ancestors had once lived in Spain and Portugal. The Sephardic Jews developed a high cultural life in these lands of their origin, known in the annals of Jewish history, of course, as the Golden Age.

In 1492 (the year of the discovery of America, and of the banishment of the Jews from Spain in accordance with the resolution taken by the Grand Inquisitor Torquemada), Isacco da Pisa, a Jewish philanthropist who lived in Pisa, started to help Spanish refugees settle in the city. Isacco came from a family of bankers, and he founded the Monte di Pietà, a loan bank in Pisa that helped the underprivileged, one of the first of its kind in the world. I believe that among those refugees helped by Isacco da Pisa were some of my ancestors. Many other Spanish and, later, Portuguese refugees wandered from country to country for several years. Cosimo the First, Grand Duke of Tuscany, of the great Medici family, and his successor the Grand Duke Ferdinand invited a considerable number of fugitive Jews to settle in Pisa and Leghorn. The Medicis wished to promote Pisa as a commercial center, but a much larger number of immigrants preferred to remain in the neighboring town of Leghorn, which grew as an international port. It was among the Jews of Leghorn that the philanthropist Moses Montefiore, so well known in England and in the United States, and the modern painter Amedeo Modigliani were born. Other immigrants went to other Italian cities that offered more opportunities.

Because the Spanish and Portuguese refugees outnumbered the original Italian Jews, practically all Jewish congregations in Italy, including that of Pisa, became Sephardic as far as religious culture is concerned. The little congregation of Pisa reached its acme in 1881, when its members numbered 700.

In many respects the Pisan Jews were a kind of paradigm of the whole of Italian Jewry. They, like Jews throughout Italy, had become assimilated into Italian culture in a short period of time. Within their families they continued to use some Spanish and Hebrew words, but they spoke Italian like the other citizens and considered themselves Italians of the Jewish faith.

During the *Risorgimento,* the historical complex of insurrections and wars of independence that, between 1848 and 1870, led to the liberation of Italy from foreign oppression and to its unification, Italian Jews participated actively in the momentous events. They provided asylum for the great patriot Mazzini. They enrolled in the volunteer army of "The Thousand," which, under the leadership of Garibaldi, liberated the south of Italy. Cavour, the first and the ablest Italian secretary of state, who, with the concerted military efforts of Garibaldi, succeeded in unifying Italy, had several friends among the Jews.

It can be said without hesitation that after the unification of Italy, there was no other country either in Europe or in the whole world where Jews felt so well integrated into the general population. If anti-Semitism existed, it was minimal and confined to certain small circles. In this climate, needless to say, Italian Jews prospered. Many of them belonged to the upper bourgeoisie or to the intelligentsia. Although they never numbered more than 80,000, their impact on Italian life was considerable, especially in the cities of Ferrara, Milan, Turin, Venice, Rome, and Trieste. They especially excelled in the field of mathematics. Every student of higher mathematics knows the names of such innovators as Tullio Levi Civita, Giuseppe Peano, and Vito Volterra. Italy was the first Christian country to have a Jew as premier, Luigi Luzzatti, who held that office in 1910 and 1911. In fact, until Mussolini began to yield to Hitler's wishes, all had gone well between the Italian Jews and the rest of the Italians. But the man who on August 28, 1934 had rejected German racism with a grandiloquent sentence—"Thirty centuries of history allow us to look with sovereign disdain and piety on certain theories followed north of the Alps"—four years later began to imitate the Nazi leader with an anti-Semitism that, while not as fanatic as the German's, was nevertheless unequivocal. Many Jews began to prepare to leave Italy. I was one of them.

Pardo was not the only person I went to say goodbye to. Another was Pietro, my first patient.

I have already mentioned that a short time before I left Italy, I had been graduated from the medical school of Pisa. Although I had not formally begun postgraduate psychiatric training, I had written my thesis (required in European medical schools) in neuropsychiatry, and I had spent a considerable amount of time in the psychiatric department of the university. This department was directed by a person from whom I learned much neurology, Professor Giuseppe Ayala, who, as I discovered later on my arrival in America, was well known on this side of the Atlantic, too, for his studies on brain tumors. Professor Ayala was an excellent neurologist, but because of the way medical education was organized at that time, he was obliged to teach psychiatry as well, a field he considered inferior to neurology. Psychiatry thus was badly neglected in his department. Although only a student, I had read

Freud and the works of the Italian psychoanalyst Edoardo Weiss, and I was already a firm believer in psychotherapy and psychoanalysis. Professor Ayala was very liberal, and in spite of my student status he allowed me to choose and treat some patients with psychotherapy. I chose to treat Pietro as my very first patient. It is because of his special relationship to me that he is the only person in this book to whom I refer by first name only.

Pietro was a very warm and interesting person. It is not difficult to understand why I selected him without hesitation. He was suffering from a severe type of phobia called *agoraphobia*. He was afraid to leave home, to walk on the streets, and especially to cross squares. At that time the only treatment available at the Institute for this type of illness consisted of changing the environment and prescribing some sedatives and some so-called tonic medicines like neurophosphates, allegedly supposed to strengthen the nervous system.

Pietro was intelligent and sensitive, and he suspected that except for the change of environment, the treatment was worthless. With the permission of Professor Ayala I attempted psychotherapy along psychoanalytic lines. I tried to understand and explain Pietro's conflicts, and in spite of my lack of adequate preparation, he gradually improved. Although I could not hope to achieve a complete recovery, I put a great deal of zeal, zest, and devotion into this, which was the first therapeutic attempt of my life and an arduous one. Pietro's fears diminished to the point where he could leave the Institute and dare to walk on the street, at first with the help of a bicycle, which he did not ride but took along as if it were a companion who could give him support and reassurance. Later he was able to venture out without any help. Pietro was a devoted husband and father, and a devout Catholic. He was very grateful to me. When I went to say goodbye to him and told him that I had to leave Italy in a hurry, he gave me the names and addresses of relatives in London whom I could contact in case of need. That need was indeed to arise. When I left

Italy, I stayed for a few weeks first in Switzerland and then in London, waiting for available room on a ship bound for America.

When I returned to Pisa after the war to see my parents, who unbelievably, miraculously, had escaped death, one of the first persons I met on the main street was Pietro. He was shocked and exuberantly happy to see me. He rushed to tell me many things about the terrible conditions in Pisa during the war. Since my parents had escaped from the city during that period and could not give me much information, I was eager to get it from Pietro.

The summer of 1944 had been bad beyond imagining. The city had been relentlessly bombed by the Allies, and the Germans, who had taken over that part of Italy after the fall of Mussolini, were vexing and terrorizing the Italian populace. They could not forgive the Italians for the fact that their new government, residing in the south, was now on the side of the Allies. The Germans knew very well that although the north of Italy was officially with Germany, the hearts of the majority of the people were not with them. During the last part of the war Pisa had almost become a ghost town, especially during the battle of the Arno River. The Arno divides Pisa into two parts, north and south. During this battle the Germans were north of the Arno, occupying a large part of Pisa, including the old city with its major monuments. The Allies were in the southern part. To escape the bombing, more than two-thirds of the population fled the city and spread out into villages in the surrounding country. Only a skeleton of administrative offices were still functioning, and only a small number of people had for various reasons decided to remain in their homes at any cost. Pietro was among them.

I asked Pietro why he had remained in the city. Without any hesitation he told me that it was because of his illness. After I left Italy in 1939, he continued to do well for some time, but unfortunately the illness came back toward the end of 1942. When the violence of the war quickened and most people evacuated the city, he was among the few who remained behind. He felt almost stuck to the place where he lived, and he could not go beyond the block where his home was located. The fear caused by the neurosis was stronger than the fear of the dangers of the war. He lived not too far from the leaning tower and the other historical monuments. At first he convinced himself that both sides would respect the town's great art treasures and the mementos of its and Italy's glorious past. But soon it was quite clear that whether or not the armed forces of both sides wanted to respect the monuments, they were not so accurate in aiming at their targets. Many nearby houses were demolished, even on the block where he lived; several people were killed and many injured. Since he was compelled by his phobias to remain no farther than a block away from where he lived, after each bombing he would rush out to free people trapped in the nearby ruins, and he saved several lives.

Thus, at the end of the war, not only was he alive and safe, but he had also become a hero and was decorated for acts of heroism. His illness was then treated by a psychotherapist, and Pietro recovered. He is well now and lives somewhere in Italy. He continues to be the same warm, compassionate, and intelligent person he revealed himself to be when I first met him. In spite of his modesty and the absence of any desire to attain glory, his illness made him become a hero. It seemed to have bestowed on him a magic immunity from danger, so that he is still with us to tell his story of the war period and of the other many experiences of his rich life. I shall refer to him from time to time in the telling of my main story, the story of the other sufferer from phobias, Giuseppe Pardo Roques.

Afternoon and
Early Evening of July 31

On June 10, 1940, Mussolini, convinced Germany would win, declared war on the Allies and put Italy on the side of Germany. As he explained to his son-in-law Galeazzo Ciano, he "needed a few thousand dead so that he could sit at the peace table" as a victor. But the war proved disastrous for him. In the fall of 1942 the Americans landed in North Africa. On July 10, 1943, the Allies landed in Sicily and started their conquest of the island. Everybody in Italy now could foresee defeat. Most members of the Gran Consiglio, the highest order of the Fascist party hierarchy, formed a conspiracy with the help of the king. They convened in the night between July 24 and 25 in the presence of Mussolini and voted to depose him. He would have to resign and return some powers to the king. The following day the king had Mussolini arrested and appointed Marshal Badoglio head of the government. On July 28 Badoglio announced to the people that the Fascist party had been dissolved, and on September 8 he announced that Italy had signed an armistice with the Allies.

The Italians were jubilant. They poured into the streets of cities, towns, and villages to sing, dance, and drink. But the joy did not last long. The Germans were furious. They denounced the Italians as traitors, traitors to their German ally and to the cause of Fascism. Even Badoglio had promised the German ambassador to continue the war on the side of Germany after the fall of Mussolini, all the while secretly negotiating with the Allies the surrender of Italy. On September 11 the Germans occupied Rome. On September 12, in a very skillful operation, they liberated Mussolini from an almost inaccessible place of incarceration in the mountains of Gran Sasso, occupied northern and central Italy, and reinstated Mussolini as the head of the government. Only the south of Italy was under the official Badoglio government and the king. In the central and northern parts the Germans ruled, either directly or through the intermediary of the Fascist government and the newly founded Republican Fascist party. This new Fascist government proclaimed Italy no longer a kingdom but a republic and reaffirmed loyalty to Germany.

Nine months earlier, Winston Churchill had said, "The paramount task before us is . . . to strike at the underbelly of the Axis in effective strength and in the shortest time." But the shortest time proved to be long. The Germans put up strong resistance. Cassino, along the Gustave line, fell on May 17, 1944, after very heavy losses on both sides. Rome, no longer well defended, was occupied by the Allies on June 4, 1944. President Roosevelt was jubilant. He commented, "The first Axis capital is in our hands. One down and two to go."

But in Italy the march toward victory was to prove very long. Two days after the fall of Rome came D-Day. The Allies invaded Normandy and began to concentrate their main effort on the northern European front. The German troops in Italy under the command of Marshal Kesselring gradually withdrew to form the Gothic line, a line of defense that extended from the Tyrrhenian Sea to the Adriatic Sea, near Rimini.

During their occupation of part of Italy, the Germans were kept busy by the vicissitudes of war, but they did not relinquish their customary activities, especially their onslaught against the Jews. The Jewish population of Italy, harassed and persecuted by the Italian Fascists, naturally found itself in a far worse condition when the Germans took over.

From the time of the fall of Mussolini (July 25, 1943) to the end of the war (May 8, 1945) the Germans captured and deported 7,495 Italian Jews. Of these, 6,885 were murdered; only 610 returned. Continuous raids were made to capture Jews in places where they were expected to be. In Rome alone on October 16, 1943, the Germans captured 1,127 Jews, including 800 women and children, and sent them to extermination camps from which only 14 men and 1 woman returned. This was done in spite of the fact that exactly one month earlier (September 16, 1943) the Germans had promised not to molest the Jews if they delivered over fifty kilograms of gold, which they did.

On September 17, 1943, the Germans ordered the parnas of the Jewish congregation of Venice, Giuseppe Jona, to prepare a list of the names and addresses of the Venetian Jews. He was given one day. During that time he warned as many members of the Jewish community as he could reach to escape from the city and then killed himself before the Germans arrived to demand the list. In spite of his efforts, more than 300 Venetian Jews were captured, including those who were in the Jewish home for the aged. In Ferrara, on November 14, 150 Jews were taken, and not fewer than 710 were captured in Trieste between October and January 1944.

Although communication was extremely difficult, and nobody could know for sure what had happened to his fellow Jews, all Jews were fully conscious of the danger. Some moved away and went to places where they were not known; some were hidden in the homes of Christian friends; some were permitted to enter monasteries and convents pretending to be monks and nuns; some were allowed to pose as patients in psychiatric hospitals; some, like my parents, moved from village to village in the mountains, pretending to have been evacuated from the cities because of the bombings. On the whole, Italian Catholics not associated with the Fascist party tried to save Jews. But for the Jews there was always the danger of being recognized and reported to the police or to the Germans, either by Fascists or by merely malevolent or vindictive people. Every Jew tried to save himself by whatever means he could devise.

This, however, was not so of Giuseppe Pardo Roques. From the beginning of the war he had remained in his home in Pisa, on Sant' Andrea Street. There with him were six people, all Jews, who had asked to be his guests for the duration of the war. These seven did not leave town, nor hide in the country, nor disguise their Jewish identity.

On September 13, 1943, five days after Badoglio announced the armistice and the unconditional surrender of Italy, two visitors came to see Pardo and urged him and his guests to leave. One of them was Dr. Elio Arieti, my father, and the other was the attorney Guido De Cori.[1] My father and Mr. De Cori tried to impress on Pardo that the news of the armistice was not good for the part of Italy still under German occupation, and especially not for the Jews. The jubilation the people had manifested in the streets at the news of the surrender was not justified as long as the Germans continued to occupy that part of Italy. Pardo and his guests should leave at once, the visitors said. Their urgent advice fell on deaf ears. Pardo referred vaguely to his being ill and too old to try to find a hiding place. The others would not leave without him. And so, almost a year later, in July 1944, Pardo and his guests were still there on Sant' Andrea Street. Neither the Germans nor the Fascists nor the bombings had induced them to move. With the exception of one—Cesare Gallichi—Pardo and his guests were intelligent and well-informed people who had experienced life in various rich ways. It is true that, again with the exception of Cesare

1. Guido De Cori has provided me with much information for the preparation of this book.

Gallichi, they were all of advanced age, but not so advanced as to be considered decrepit or physically incapacitated. Pardo was not even sixty-nine; Cesare Gallichi was forty-nine.

A vast literature has already been devoted to the agonizing question of why so many Jews did not do more to save themselves. Giorgio Bassani, in *The Garden of the Finzi-Continis,* portrayed the psychological unwillingness of a wealthy old Italian Jewish family to admit the very existence of danger. According to Bassani they did not even make a strong conscious effort to deny the danger; they simply lived as if it did not exist. Undoubtedly this protective mechanism occurs in some persons who visualize themselves as possible victims. But in the case of Pardo and his six guests, after so much evidence to the contrary, such a denial would have been impossible. If a need to deny had taken hold of these people, it must have had more complex roots.

Other people have attributed this state of passivity of would-be victims to a demoralization that prevents revolt or even suicidal acts of rebellion. In any case, Italian Jews were denied such kinds of rebellious action. Being so few and so scattered through the country, they could not have organized even the smallest armed resistance. Others have attributed the inaction of many Jews to a pervading feeling of helplessness—a paralyzing feeling derived from the conviction that there is nothing one can do to save oneself. But this feeling of paralyzing helplessness did not exist among Italian Jews. Unlike the Jews of, say, Poland or Hungary, most of the Italian Jews in the end did succeed in one way or another in saving themselves. Out of a total of approximately 40,000 who had remained in Italy after the start of official anti-Semitism, 7,495 were captured and deported. Although the number provides no occasion for rejoicing, it can easily be said that in terms of percentage, Italian Jews fared much better than Jews of other countries under German oppression.

Still another theory holds that no matter what the Jews or anyone knew about Fascism and Nazism, they could not conceive of the true extent of this new evil. How could anyone imagine that supposedly civilized or once-civilized nations could engage in such barbarous acts so extensively? This hypothesis seems to me plausible for the majority of European Jews. In fact, how *could* they have known? There is no comparable example in history. Caligula, Nero, and the other tyrants of antiquity, including the biblical Pharaoh, are pale figures in the practice of barbarism in comparison to Hitler. Many people refused to believe that such atrocities were possible among humans and thought that the rumors they heard about the tortures and massacres were Allied propaganda. Many Jews thought, "We may be incarcerated and obliged to work for the duration of the war, but after the war we shall be free."

But even this theory is not valid for the seven people we are considering. It was July 1944; by this time Hitler had already disclosed the previously unimaginable potentiality of evil. The tortures, the burying alive, the starvation, and the refined ways of prolonging suffering for human beings—let alone the wholesale methods for slaughtering them—were by then known throughout Europe.

In July 1944 Pisa became a major theater of war, part of what was called the Gothic line. The neighboring city of Leghorn fell to the Allies on July 19, and the announcement that Pisa had fallen was made on July 23. But the announcement was not really true. Only the part of Pisa that was south of the Arno River was in American hands. The Germans had blown up all the bridges, including the historic Ponte di Mezzo. The part of the city north of the Arno was still under the control of the Germans and their Italian satellites.

The Arno River, which had been an important instrument of war in the twelfth and thirteenth centuries when the great maritime republic of Pisa conquered Corsica and Sardinia and her ships extended their activities to the most remote lands of the Mediterranean Sea, had been left in a state of placid tranquillity for over half a millenium. After the Pisan fleet was disastrously defeated in 1284 by the Genoese, the republic and her river might at least partially have returned to their joint former splendor had not yet another misfortune intervened. The Tyrrhenian Sea, on whose shore the city was located, withdrew, leaving the city several miles inland. Pisa lost access to the sea, and its naval and political power crumbled.

Eventually the widow of the sea, as D'Annunzio called Pisa, transformed the streets along the banks of the river from naval installations to *lungarni,* quiet riverside streets where the passage of time seemed to have tamed history forever and created a vision of peace and beauty—a place where poets from many lands found inspiration. Some of these poets come quickly to mind because they are so dear to all English-speaking people of the world —Byron, Shelley, and Browning; others are revered because of the important role they played in Italian literature, such as Leopardi, Giusti, Carducci, Pascoli, and D'Annunzio. And then, of course, there is that controversial poet of our own day, the mention of whose name can still stir passions, the author of the "Pisan Cantos."

But by July 1944 every vestige of poetry and peace was gone. The violence of war awakened the river from its six centuries of sleep. The Americans from the south and the Germans from the north were engaged for a time in preventing any crossing of the Arno, in either direction, at any cost—even the destruction of the city. But this frantic activity lasted only a short time; after the Americans had secured their occupation of the southern part of the city, a strange kind of lull set in. The Americans south of Pisa and the British south of Florence gave no sign of any immediate intention of crossing the Arno. This lull, to be sure, was frequently interrupted by sniper fire from both sides of the river and by the rumbling of artillery.

Why didn't the Allies cross the river, since they knew that the overwhelming majority of the population was eagerly waiting for the day of liberation? Among those waiting were Pardo and his guests. Pardo's home was only three hundred yards north of the Arno River.

There was no doubt that the German High Command had ordered Marshal Kesselring to convince the Allies that German might was not completely broken. His troops were told to resist, using every available method and utilizing natural defenses as much as possible. If the Gothic line remained intact, Germany would still be protected from the south, with the north of Italy in German hands. The Gothic line included the mountains below the Po Valley. If the Germans were forced to abandon that line of defense, they presumably could be forced to cross the Brenner Pass, leave Italy, and expose Germany to a southern attack. This was German reasoning. The fact was, however, that German power was crumbling and that the Arno River was not a formidable natural defense at all. It is narrow, and in summer months it becomes so shallow at some points between Florence and Pisa that people can cross it by foot.

If in time of war people show themselves capable of barbarity, they can also show a marked humanity and respect for culture. Such respect was found in the Allied Command, which was about to invade the most historic and artistic part of Tuscany. The British were unwilling to subject Florence to the devastation of war—Florence, where many of the world's greatest treasures of art had been preserved since the Renaissance. So were the Americans who had reached the Arno. The decision to pursue the Germans and to fight them in the streets of the northern part of Pisa would have meant accepting the destruction of all the historic monuments, bringing on, among other things, the fall of the leaning tower. Even if the Germans had abandoned the north of Pisa to the Americans, they could have bombed the city from Mount Pisano and the surrounding hills, jeopardizing the existence of all the monuments.

Meanwhile, during that same month of July, far away from the Gothic line on safe American ground, I was avidly reading the news every day in the *New York Times* and the *Herald Tribune*. When I read that the Americans had not advanced to the northern part of Pisa because they did not want to damage the famous square and especially the leaning tower, I was skeptical at first. I thought that military strategy would overrule all other considerations, and that perhaps what the newspapers were reporting was a cover-up. But eventually I accepted the reports at face value. After all, many people did consider the main square of my hometown to be the most beautiful in the world. There the cathedral, the baptistry, the tower, and the ancient cemetery, as "marmoreal giants," had for many centuries stood the test of time and the fury of men. And for century after century the majesty of learning had joined with the sublimity of art in that square. When the sea withdrew and her military power vanished, Pisa devoted herself to learning and in 1343 founded her famous university. The more the sea receded, the more culture advanced; the more political power declined, the more learning grew.

In that square the geniuses of the centuries, philosophers and poets, sculptors and architects, physicians and mathematicians, had strolled around and met one another—had talked and even made scientific experiments. I carried around a vision of that square; in my mind's eye I used to see Leonardo Fibonacci, who, at the beginning of the thirteenth century, gave the concept of *zero* to the Western world. I could visualize him in the act of explaining to his fellow Pisans that zero is by no means zero, but a great numerical concept by which nothingness is transformed into a numerical entity, the figure o. Although zero as a symbol had been previously invented by the Babylonians and the Indians, it was not known even by such culturally developed people as the Greeks, the Romans, and Europeans up to the early Renaissance. Leonardo Fibonacci had learned the concept from the Arabs, refined it, and introduced it into Europe together with algebra. I could imagine him explaining to the amazed crowd that what stands for nothingness is also a device that creates the decimal numeration. "Add two, three, six zeros," he would say to the Pisans, "and you have 100, 1,000, 1,000,000. What a capacity for growth have these symbols of nothingness when put one next to the other!"

And I could imagine, strolling in the square about 1650, the great Malpighi, who discovered the blood capillaries and the corpuscles of Malpighi in the kidneys. I could imagine the greatest of all Pisans, Galileo, when, at the age of seventeen, he saw a lamp swinging in the cathedral and formulated the principle of the pendulum. Or later, when he dropped objects from the top of the leaning tower and discovered that, contrary to expectation, a feather and a stone reached the ground at the same time. Because of the leaning of the tower he could determine that the acceleration of the falling bodies decreased consistently with their angle of inclination. Historians of physics consider these experiments the beginning of mechanics and of modern science. And certain parochial Pisans might stretch their capacity for wishful thinking and conclude that had the tower been straight, modern science would have had no chance to develop. At all events, what is beyond doubt is that the leaning tower seems, when one gazes at it, to be a feat of magic. Even straight, it would be a great work of art. But the fact that it has maintained its hazardous existence for centuries adds wonder to wonder. Its architectural harmony combines with its imperfection to create an unpremeditated miracle.

In reflecting on the tower I have occasionally thought that similar paradoxical combinations can in rare cases appear in human beings, too. Moses, a stutterer, became the most powerful voice of his people; the deaf Beethoven wrote sublime melodies. Could it not also be that from some unusual endowed persons who are mentally ill we can learn some secrets of human existence?

Safe on American soil, I was glad that the Allies were trying to spare the square, and especially the tower. I was not aware that this meant prolongation of suffering for the people awaiting liberation in the northern part of Pisa. I was not aware that among them, and in a particularly dangerous position, was my revered old friend Pardo and his guests.

The lull that followed the American occupation of Pisa south of the Arno seemed very long and surprised many people. On the afternoon of July 31 life had begun to appear calm again in the northern part of Pisa. The intense summer heat also helped to induce a somnolent, easy feeling.

In Italy it is customary, especially during the summer months, to take a daily siesta in the early hours of the afternoon. The early afternoon of July 31, then, found Giuseppe Pardo Roques and his six guests so engaged. Only Silvia Bonanni, the maid who had been in the Pardo Roques' home for many years, could not rest. She kept hearing the words of her niece—who was not actually her niece but the daughter of a close friend—who had come to see her. The girl had come quietly in the morning, taken Silvia aside, and told her in an anguished whisper, "Auntie, Auntie, Mother thinks you shouldn't stay in this home a minute longer. Get away! Get away!" Her agitation grew with each subsequent word.

"Signor Pardo needs me," Silvia replied. "I cannot leave him. They gave me special permission to stay." Silvia referred to a permit that so-called Aryan people had to obtain in order to work as domestics in Jewish homes. Since Mussolini had adopted Hitler's anti-Semitism, one of the many laws imposed was that no Aryan could work in the home of a Jew. However, before the Germans had actually taken over after the fall of Mussolini, some of these laws were not strictly enforced and ways to circumvent them had been found. Because Pardo was sick and needed assistance, he had been allowed by the Italian Fascists to retain his Christian maid. After the fall of Mussolini, this concession was revoked, but no one had informed Pardo.

"Things are different now. What if they come? Mother said you should quit at once. Tell him. After all, there are other women in the house." The girl referred to Ida Gallichi and Cesira Levi, who, along with their husbands, were among Pardo's guests.

"They are old, and they, too, need me. I cannot leave, and I will not leave. Nobody will hurt me."

"Auntie, what makes you so sure?"

"I have a strong feeling that tomorrow our fears will be over. We are going to be liberated. The Americans are already in Pisa, on the other side of the Arno. Go, reassure Mother. Get away fast. Don't *you* stay here!" The girl left. Why did Silvia add her last remark? Normally she would not have dismissed the girl so abruptly. Was she, too, in a state of alarm? Was she about to experience panic, in addition to the other feeling she expressed, that liberation was imminent? Or did she refuse to acknowledge danger because then she would have to do what was unacceptable to her—quit at once?

Nor could Pardo rest that afternoon. When he heard Silvia moving around, he got up and went into the kitchen. When she saw him so unexpectedly, she started.

"Silvia," Pardo told her, "today while you were giving us lunch, you seemed to me to be feeling grave."

"I did not know I was."

"I know that your friend's daughter came to tell you to leave."

"I won't leave."

"You must follow your friend's advice."

"I must decide for myself."

"My guests and I are Jewish; you are not. Put yourself in a safe spot. Go away, together with Giovanna and Alice." These were two other women who helped Silvia. Giovanna was the widow of Pasquino, who had been Pardo's chauffeur for many years. When Pasquino died, Giovanna had remained as a helper in Pardo's household, with Alice, her younger sister.

"There is no place safer than this, Signor Pardo. The Nazis, the Fascists, and the bombs have not touched us. The Americans are almost here, just on the other side of the Arno, and *now* you want us to leave?"

"Silvia, you must go with Giovanna and Alice."

"Only if you come with us. Signor Pardo, tell your friends to come, too. We'll go to the country, to the village I come from."

"My guests don't want to leave. They, too, feel safe here, as you do. But I must convince them. They must go even if I don't. They're resting now. I'll talk to them when they get up."

One by one they got up. Some of them had rested as usual, as if that afternoon had been a normal summer day. Others had had only a short nap; some underlying, aching feeling had kept them from rest. One by one they gathered in the large living room on the main floor. First came the oldest, Teofilo Gallichi, with his wife Ida and their son Cesare; then Doctor Dario, brother of Teofilo, an old family doctor of Pardo's; then Ernesto Levi and his wife Cesira. Except for the Levis, who came from Genoa, all were Pisan Jews. Every afternoon they gathered in that room to talk, listen to the radio if there was electricity, or go out for a walk in the beautiful garden. When they were all together, Pardo felt the moment had come to talk to them.

"My friends," he said, "we have gone through many dangers together. We have counted the days, the hours, until the Americans arrive. Eight days ago we heard the Allies were in Pisa, but we do not know what has happened since. The river has not been crossed, and we are still among Fascists and Nazis. We do not know how long this lull will last, maybe till tomorrow, maybe till next year. This suspension of hostilities is a warning. You must leave at once."

One by one they answered, as they had already done on many occasions. They had not noticed Pardo's special alarm. So this time they answered in their customary manner, rather slowly, and with an abundance of words—a habit that a certain class of people had retained from the period of the end of the nineteenth century and were zealously sticking to as an emblem of the glorious past. These people retained a special kind of formality not just in their manner but in the particular words they chose to speak. Contrary to the way such speech would be interpreted today, this was a sign not of distance but precisely of friendship and closeness, the identification card of a group of people who wished to preserve the niceties of life.

Teofilo was the first to respond. He was a retired accountant, almost seventy-eight, and as the oldest of the group he felt he should be the first to talk. "Giuseppe, we feel so safe here, and now you advise us to go. Nobody has molested us, and it is more than a year since the Germans took over. There is no certainty about what will happen to us if we leave. We may be arrested at the next corner. We are not sure here either, but here we are together, and together we shall live or die. Personally, I believe that if the Germans wanted to get us, they would have already done so. We have good reason to feel safe here with you, Giuseppe."

Pardo replied, "That's what disturbs me, Teofilo, that you feel safe. If I have contributed to this feeling, I want to warn you, because it may be a feeling that deceives all of you."

Dario, the doctor, who inclined more toward practicality than Teofilo, said, "Giuseppe, you have been generous with everybody, even with the Fascists before they became allied with Hitler. The local Fascists and the police, I am sure, still extort money from you to keep quiet. Let's be frank; that's why they do not molest us. No matter where we went, we would not have this special arrangement. We would be immediately recognized, and we would find ourselves in a much worse situation."

Dario was in some respects correct. The local chiefs of the Fascist party had been extorting money from Pardo from time to time. There had been nothing for him to do but to go along with their demands. And it was obvious that whatever he gave them was no guarantee of protection.

Pardo replied, "We cannot rely on money. You know what happened in Rome, after the fifty kilograms of gold."

Cesare Gallichi, the youngest of the group, nodded in assent. He was about to say something about the unreliability of money, but hesitated and stopped. Pardo continued. "If we stay together, we can certainly be recognized here or elsewhere; but if each of us goes his own way, we may have a chance."

"No, no," said Cesare Gallichi, "we do not want to separate." The idea of being without the others scared him. Poor Cesare Gallichi, although adult (he was forty-nine years old), acted like a child; and his limited mental capacity contrasted with that of the rest of the group. In childhood he had suffered from meningitis, which had left him somewhat impaired. He was not mentally defective, but he lacked initiative, and even as an adult he depended on his parents, Teofilo and Ida. His sister Lucia was married and not with them. Although he was generally not listened to as a competent person, what he said this time found acceptance in the whole group. Nobody was inclined to part from the others; together they seemed to protect one another. They nodded in assent. Cesare smiled with satisfaction.

Cesira Levi felt she should be the first woman to reply to Pardo. She said, "Since this trouble started, I have never felt as secure as in this house. Whatever the reason, I feel safe. Before I came to Pisa to be in your home with Ernesto, I was so troubled, I could not cope with my anxiety. Ernesto can tell you. One day I had the urge to go to the German headquarters and say, 'Here I am, a Jewish woman. Dispose of me as you want. I no longer want to wait for my death, day by day.' Ernesto stopped me. But since I have been here, with all of you, I no longer worry. Whatever will be, will be. I even have a good time in this house. I enjoy helping our Christian neighbors when they come to get water here. This could happen only in Pisa." Cesira referred to the fact that from the beginning of that unusually hot summer, the drought and the bombing of some aqueducts and pipes had made water very scarce in the city. But in the garden of Pardo's home there was a well that seemed to have an inexhaustible supply of water. Every morning many neighbors, all Christians, would come with containers to get the precious liquid. It made no difference to them that it came from a Jewish well.

Ernesto Levi said, "I fully support my wife. I helped her the day she wanted to surrender to the Nazis. Now she helps all of us with her hopeful view. When every door was closed to us, we came here, and this door was open, and this home has been a safe place, in spite of everything."

Pardo again intervened. "I am not requesting that you leave. You are my dear guests, and you can remain as long as I am alive. But you must know that what you get here is hospitality, not security. The Allies have stopped their march. Every time the doorbell rings or somebody knocks, we shall be jolted. We shall think, 'There they are. They have come to take us away.'"

At this, Ida Gallichi started to talk in quite an effusive manner. She said, "My husband was the first to talk, and I want to be the last. I am an old woman, and I have seen many things in my life. With the exception of Cesira, I think all of you are wrong, including you, Giuseppe. This time you are wrong, too. I shall make myself say what each of us felt inside and yet nobody said. Giuseppe, you tell us that you give us hospitality but not security. You are wrong through and through. *You give us security.* If we were not safe here, would we be alive today, after a year of German domination? You, Dario, spoke about the money given to the Fascists, but they could come and take all the money they want. Money has nothing to do with it. No bombing, no lack of food and water, no Nazi, no Fascist has imperiled this holy home. I wish my daughter Lucia were here. I worry for her, not for us. Giuseppe, you are not just our host. You are our protector, and your personality has made even this period of time pleasant. When people as old as Teofilo and I prepare for the grave, we learn faster than ever before. You have been our teacher. But most of all, you have prayed for us. The synagogue is two blocks from here, but this home is an extension of the synagogue. God must be with us; God must guide you, our host. The Divine Presence must be here and surrounding us because of you, our parnas."

At this point Ernesto Levi, who had not spoken much before, perhaps under the influence of a memory of his bar mitzvah started to say loudly, scanning the syllables, "Because of the Shekhinah that rests in you! The Shekhinah!"

For readers who are not acquainted with the meaning of this Hebrew word, I shall attempt an explanation of this not easily definable concept. In rabbinical literature most of the time Shekhinah means the Divine Presence, or the immanence of God in the world. At other times it means the presence of God at a given place or in the actions of a given person. The rabbis have used the term to indicate the Divine Presence in the life of some human beings who possess *Ru'ah ha-Kodesh,* a divine spirit or perhaps divine emanation. According to Encyclopaedia Judaica, "the Shekhinah is commonly associated with the charismatic personality and is thought to rest on specific outstanding individuals."[2]

It is in this last meaning that Ernesto used the word in talking to Pardo.

"The Shekhinah that rests in you," said Ernesto once more.

"The Shekhinah," repeated Ida, and after her, Cesira, Cesare, and even Teofilo. Only Dario, the doctor, kept quiet.

Pardo was pale and trembling. He was silent for a few minutes. Then he decided that the moment had come to unlock his personal drama. And he spoke again at length. He said, "What you have just told me is serious. I had not expected it. What you have said requires me to tell you things I had never intended to discuss with you, close to one another as we have all become. What I am going to tell you is no secret, but now I can talk to

2. *Encyclopaedia Judaica* (Jerusalem: Keter Publishing House, Ltd., 1971), vol. 14, p. 1351.

you about it. You have attributed to me a special gift. And yet the truth is that in many respects I am much less gifted than the average man in the street.

"I know that you know about my illness, the illness that has caused such a narrowing of my life, not to mention gossip and ridicule, and has shadowed my whole existence. I live, trembling, with a totally irrational fear of animals, especially of dogs. I also have a fear of the fear itself. This is what prevents me from facing the real danger. Had I not felt this sick fear constantly, I would not be here; I would be far away. What you call a special gift is illness. But you are not affected by it. You can go. Go, go away. I have been told that at times I hypnotize people. Am I hypnotizing you to stay? It seems to me that I try my very best to convince you to leave."

Ida became excited and replied quickly, as if she had prepared the answer long ago. "You don't hypnotize us. We use our judgment. You say that you are afflicted by false fears. And I say, blessed be your false fears. We have remained safe, here, protected by your fears."

Cesira added, "God may use even sick fears for a good cause."[3]

Turning to Pardo, Ernesto said in a serious and steady voice, "What you call your power to hypnotize comes from the Shekhinah. I believe your illness, too, is part of it."

Pardo asked, "Even if you risk the danger of dying for it?"

Ernesto replied, "I believe that when Shekhinah rests in some people it may require illness and death." He had once again begun with the modest "I believe," but his belief was instantly appropriated by the whole group and transformed into something stronger than a mere opinion.

Pardo gave up. Clearly he could not persuade them to leave. Perhaps among all the contradictory emotions coursing through

3. Such an interpretation sometimes seems plausible. Take the case of Pietro, who was aided by his irrational fears to help others and to save several lives.

him, he could even recognize a certain relief and pleasure that they had decided to stay. Love and loyalty of this kind are difficult to resist, even when cold logic dictates the need for a different kind of response. Added to them, of course, was that primal hope for survival that persists in the spirit of practically every human being alive.

Pardo called Silvia and told her that that evening they wanted to have an early supper. "Let's have some wine," he said. "Tonight we must have some kind of celebration."

Silvia asked whether the case of French champagne that had been down in the cellar for a long time should be opened.

"No," said Pardo, "that we shall save for a bigger occasion. We have two bottles of Orvieto wine, and they will do." The champagne, of course, was to be reserved for the day of liberation.

Silvia, with Giovanna and Alice, went through the house closing all the shutters. From the beginning of the war, the authorities had ruled that, in addition to putting blue paper on the windowpanes, citizens should close all shutters so that no light could help the enemy identify locations. Alice and Giovanna also lit a few kerosene lamps. Very little electricity was available because the bombing had disconnected or destroyed the main power lines. A small amount of current from the city's local generators was available in some parts of town, but only when the Fascist radio station transmitted the High Command's official news bulletins. The friends began to get ready for supper. The women changed and freshened their toilette, as they would have done under the most normal of circumstances.

So dusk came, and as the group took their customary early evening walk in the garden, the first stars appeared. When it was time for supper, they convened in the dining room—a beautiful room in which I, too, dined a few times when I had the great honor of being invited by Signor Pardo. A mood of humor and gaiety prevailed. This mood was not a whistling in the graveyard but the genuine gaiety of a collective sense of satisfaction over the fact that a resolution, the best resolution, had been reached. There was high animation at the dinner table, held in check only by the need not to call the neighbors' attention to their presence.

That evening was, by common impulse, to be no different from all the others. Cesira said, "Giuseppe, what story are you going to tell us tonight? I hope it's going to be another one about the Pisan Jews."

Pardo was an inexhaustible source of stories, true stories, from his researches into archives, old books, and old manuscripts. He told them in a style that could be listened to equally by children, young adults, adults, or old people.

"Have I ever told you the story of Abramo Pace?"

"No," replied his listeners.

"He was a Jew living in Pisa, and what I am going to tell you took place in June or July 1709. Abramo Pace's three-year-old son was seriously ill. At that time there was a woman in Pisa who had come from Pistoia and practiced medicine in a clandestine way. She was a medicine-man, or rather, a medicine-woman. Some well-intentioned Pisan ladies, among whom was the wife of the Captain of Justice, knew of this woman and of her presumed extraordinary healing ability. They went to Abramo Pace and his wife and told them that the medicine-woman knew of excellent kinds of treatment unknown even to the professors at the university. They should by all means have her come to see the little boy.

"The Paces were willing to try anything, and the woman from Pistoia was welcomed. She examined the child and found him seriously ill. No treatment would help his little body, she thought, but she could save his soul and open for him the door of the Kingdom of Heaven, from which even an innocent baby is barred if he happens to be a Jew. She discussed this matter with the well-intentioned Pisan ladies, who encouraged her to go ahead. So later that day, she returned to the home of the Paces and asked to be left alone with the patient so that she could give him the best of all treatments. The hopeful father and mother agreed. Left alone with the child, she baptized him; then, full of happiness for having done the best deed of her life, she joined the friendly ladies who had supported her and who were waiting for her. Soon thereafter she returned to Pistoia.

"A few days later the child died, and he was buried in our Jewish cemetery. The whole matter would have ended there, except for one thing. Thieves had heard that the child of a rich Jew had died and that the parents had put precious ornaments in the grave as their last gift of love. During the night the thieves opened the grave and took whatever they thought was worth stealing. The theft was discovered and reported to the Captain of Justice, and his wife heard the news. You remember she was one of the well-intentioned ladies who had contacted the woman from Pistoia.

"The wife of the Captain of Justice had a crisis of conscience. She could not sleep at night. She knew why the body of the baby had not been left in peace. The child had been buried in the wrong cemetery. The child was a Christian. When the lady confided in her priest, he suggested that she follow what her conscience urged her to do and report the whole matter to the archbishop of Pisa, who was named Francesco Frosini. He had been head of the diocese of Pisa for seven years, and by an odd coincidence, he, too, was from Pistoia, like the healing woman. He undertook a punctilious and laborious inquiry. He interviewed each and every lady who had been involved with the affair, and they left no doubt that the woman from Pistoia had indeed baptized the child.

"The archbishop rejoiced that a soul had been saved, but he was concerned with the body, too. According to the law, he had the power to request that the child be exhumed and transferred to a Catholic cemetery, and he did so. That was what the ecclesiastic canons, supported by many similar cases, required.

"The Jews of Pisa were incensed. They appointed a delegation to see the archbishop. He listened to their indignant protests, preached calm, and said that everything would be done according to Christian justice. He spoke privately to the rabbi, who was a professor at the university, and told him that as archbishop he had no choice. He had to do what his faith required. The child would receive a sumptuous Christian funeral."

"What did the rabbi do?" asked Cesira.

"The rabbi realized that it was useless to fight. He did his best to quiet the members of the congregation, but he did not succeed with Abramo Pace. The anguished father would not be calmed. He hired lawyers, he appealed, he sent representatives to Rome to speak to the Pope. His argument was that if there had been a baptism, it had been given without his consent; moreover, there was no proof that there actually had been a baptism. There was only one witness, the woman from Pistoia, and the law says, '*Testis unis, testis nullus.*'"

"What does that mean?" asked Cesira again.

"It is a Latin formula used by lawyers," Dario rushed to explain, remembering his classical studies. "It means that if there is only one witness, his testimony is not binding."

Pardo continued. "Pace's lawyers insisted that even if the baptism had taken place, it was not valid according to the laws of the Church because only a man can baptize; a woman cannot. Poor Abramo Pace spent many years and most of his money vainly fighting this battle from Pisa to Rome, from Rome to Pisa. He could not be like the old Abramo—Abraham. He was not ready to sacrifice his son, even if the boy was no longer alive, for the sake of what appeared to him an injustice. But nothing was accomplished. Eventually this episode was lost even as a memory, and only bookworms come upon it from time to time."

Ida said, "That story makes me indignant. I think everybody acted abominably except the parents of the child. The woman had no right to baptize the child without the parents' consent. Moreover, even according to the Church the baptism was not valid. And what about the rabbi? Why did he acquiesce so easily?"

"Well," said Pardo, "I have a different point of view. Except, of course, for the thieves who robbed the grave, I believe everybody was true to himself, pursuing his own goal. Let's consider this medicine-woman from Pistoia. For her what was important was not the parents' consent—which she knew she would never obtain—but saving a soul. And the ladies she consulted were well-intentioned. For the wife of the Captain of Justice the thieves' actions were a divine warning: the child's body should not rest in the wrong cemetery. The priest, too, acted according to his beliefs, and so did the archbishop.

"As for the rabbi, he was not motivated by opportunism—that is, by the idea that it would not have been wise for a little Jewish congregation to contest the decision of the powerful Church. But after all, for him to make a great fuss about the baptism would have meant recognizing the sanctity of the baptism itself, something he did not want to do. For him the baptism had not caused the loss of a soul for the congregation of Pisa nor gained one for the Church. The child's soul was what it had always been. And why argue so much for a body?

"As for Abramo Pace and his wife, they, too, were being true to themselves. The child was theirs. They had to do anything to reacquire the little body."

Ernesto said, "Giuseppe, I have a lot of trouble accepting your reasoning. You seem to believe that everybody did the right thing, but how is that possible, since their goals and actions were so much at variance with one another? You seem to be proving that there is no such thing as one truth, but that each person has his own private truth, a view I know you do not really hold."

Pardo replied, "I believe there is only one absolute truth, but very seldom is it given to us to know it. We are like those prisoners in the cave described by Plato. Like them, we can see only shadows of the truth, but we are accountable for our deeds in proportion to the degree of our understanding."

"I have other troubles," said Dario. "I agree with what you said about everybody except the parents of the child. Don't you think it was excessive to spend almost one's whole capital to recover the body? As a physician, I strongly believe in doing everything in one's power to save a life. My philosophy is that we should never give up until the last moment. That's what I say to the families of my patients. But in this case the child was dead. What difference did it make in what cemetery he was buried?"

"That's not how Abramo Pace and his wife felt," replied Pardo. "Think of them. I don't know whether they had other children or not. My documents don't specify that point. They were grief-stricken about the death of the child, of course; then the decision of the archbishop made them feel that they had lost the child twice."

"But," said Teofilo, "even according to the Catholic Church the archbishop was wrong, because a woman cannot baptize."

"Give him credit for that," said Cesira. "At least he felt we women are equal to men, and that was long ago!"

At Cesira's remark everybody smiled, but Teofilo came again to the attack.

"No matter how you interpret the story, Giuseppe, my conclusion is that even then we Jews were mistreated. Even then!"

"It was not an ideal time," replied Pardo, "but think again of the little child. Everybody loved him, everybody wanted all of him, body and soul; everybody was willing to accept him, everybody was eager to save him. . . ." And he stopped there, because although he saw his friends rejoicing at the possibility of finding some graciousness in the year 1709, he was suddenly saddened at the thought of the contrast with the present time, when Jews were totally rejected, body and soul, with no possibility whatsoever of escape, even for the few who could submit to change.

So he left the dangerous subject and returned to joviality. The diners exchanged a few jokes, slowly eating the scarce food. The time for the Orvieto wine came. Pardo rose and proposed a toast.

"Let's drink," he said, "to the crossing of the Arno River, which will doom Fascism forever. We are a few yards from the river, and it may be given to us to be among the first to hear the Americans making that crossing."

The guests looked at each other, smiling. They could imagine themselves hearing the Americans in Sant' Andrea Street, rushing to open the door to greet them, to embrace them, or to open the windows and light all the lights if they came at night.

Pardo continued. "Whether we shall be the last to suffer or the first to enjoy freedom, we cannot know now; but one thing we know: The days of Fascism are numbered."

This brief speech pleased the group. They applauded, not by clapping their hands, because they did not want to make noise, but with nods and smiles.

"Let's talk about what we intend to do when we are liberated," said Ida.

"Let's," replied the group, and Teofilo, the oldest, drew himself up to begin speaking. Without economizing on words, he said that he had lived most of his life in Pisa, but that he still longed for the green hills surrounding his native Pistoia. He spoke about the beauty of Siena, surrounded by even greener hills. He said he would travel farther and farther into Tuscany, toward Perugia, where the Tuscan green blends with the Umbrian. How thirsty he had become for the green that lives forever!

His brother Dario said, "I will not go that far. I will go back to the hospital where I worked for many years and from which I was expelled because I was not a Fascist."

Ernesto interrupted. "Expelled because you were not a Fascist? I thought you were expelled because you were a Jew."

"No," said Dario with pride, "even when Mussolini acted as if he were a friend of the Jews, long before he adopted the official anti-Semitism, I refused to belong to the Fascist party. They invited me several times to join, but I always refused. So eventually I was asked to resign as chief of the department of internal medicine of Santa Chiara Hospital."

"Good for you," said Cesira. "You have my admiration."

"Don't think it was an easy thing to do," continued Dario. "Several years have passed, but the hospital is the same as I organized it, almost with the identical staff. Yes, I'll go right back. The nurses, the attendants, and some chronic patients will come to greet me as soon as they see me. They will smile; they will say nothing. They will act as if nothing had happened. The nurse who always worked with me will go to the closet to get my white gown, which all these years had been kept there with my name on it; and she will hand it to me . . . as if nothing had happened."

Ernesto said, "Cesira and I have talked about this. We shall leave Genoa and come to live in Pisa. But we shall not forget the place that we always wanted to visit, Jerusalem. If we are well, next year Cesira and I will go to Jerusalem. We still have some wine left, and I propose a second toast. Next year in Jerusalem."

The group repeated in Hebrew, "*Leshana habaah b'yerusha-laim.*" And they raised their glasses filled with the translucent white wine, and some of their glasses had begun to make the beautiful tinkling sound of clinking crystal when another strident sound arrested their arms, kept them suspended in the air, while everyone turned pale and mute. The doorbell rang.

Just that suddenly truth, lurking outside, showed its ugly face and rang down the curtain on their little scene of warmth. Who would ring that way in the dark of night with war raging? Who would come to a Jew's home at this hour, breaking the curfew? Fascists? Nazis? The Gestapo? The Italian republican police? A cold silence now hung in the room. The bell rang again.

Silvia, the maid, said in a tremulous voice, "I'll go to open the door."

"No," Cesare said firmly. "I am the youngest; I'll go." Everyone was astonished. This simpleton, this creature incapable of taking the initiative, understood that it was up to him to face the new danger and to act immediately. Nobody stopped him; nobody spoke. They heard Cesare open the door and say "Oh," but in a warm, reassuring voice. Everyone sighed with relief. Whoever the unexpected caller was, he was someone not to be feared. Cesare reappeared with a tall young man of about thirty-five.

"Angelo!" exclaimed Pardo with joy when he recognized Angelo Luzzatto, a Jew who had lived in Pisa as a boy and had moved to Parma. Smiles returned to the faces of Pardo and his guests, but Angelo appeared to be restrained, as if he wanted to join them and yet was hesitant.

"Join us," said Pardo, inviting Angelo to sit at the table. "You must drink, too. We are toasting the demise of Fascism."

Angelo replied, "That toast is premature. I am glad to see all of you alive and well, yet I was hoping that you would be undercover. When I heard no answer to my first ring of the bell, I rejoiced at the thought that you had gone to a safer spot, though I wanted to see you so much, Giuseppe."

"What do you mean?" asked Ernesto.

"In the north of Italy Jews are being arrested wherever they are found, and their homes are being raided. Many of them have been deported. We don't know where. They have done that in Tuscany, too."

"How do you know?"

"You remember Eugenio Calò? The one from Pisa who married Caterina Lombroso and has been living in Florence?"

"Of course we know Eugenio. Have they taken him?"

"No, no, he was away from home. They have taken his pregnant wife and his three little children. Nobody knows where they have been sent."

Teofilo said, "It is too late for us to move. We have considered all the possibilities, and we have decided that it is better for us to stay."

Angelo said, "I shall leave after I have spoken to Giuseppe. I regret scaring you, but I cannot share your views."

"There is something you have not told us," said Pardo.

When Angelo saw that Pardo had seen through him, he was no longer able to hold back his tears, and through sobs he managed to say, "They have taken my wife."

Pardo put his arm around Angelo's shoulders.

"I went back to my apartment after I had been away only a short time," Angelo continued, "and I couldn't find Bice. A neighbor came to me and whispered, 'The Germans were here. They took her away. Get away quickly.' He and his wife did not let me stay even for a few minutes. I couldn't think. He said, 'Go, go! Don't stay in Parma, where everybody knows you are a Jew.' I left, and now I tell you the same thing. Leave Pisa right away.'"

Affectionately, still with his arm around Angelo's shoulders, Pardo asked him, "Is Liana safe?" Liana was Angelo's daughter and his only child.

"Yes," Angelo replied. "Fortunately we sent her to England before the war started." The relief at this was great, but not great enough to compensate for the other news.

The six guests started to talk among themselves. They felt friendly toward Angelo and compassionate, but they were not grateful to him. He had broken the spell. Before he came, they had convinced themselves that Pardo's home was a safe place. Angelo had shattered that illusion. What should they do? Where should they go? What hiding place could they find? The night, the war, the Fascists, the Nazis, the police, the collaborators with the oppressors, the hostility of the world—too much to contend with. Thus, it was not difficult for them once more to come to the conclusion that at least for the present the best thing to do was to stay where they were. They thought they would stay for one or two more days. In the meantime they would think about where to go, although they had already thought a lot about it without finding a solution.

It was still early in the evening, but none of the guests felt in a talkative mood any more, and each of them was ready to retire. Moreover, Angelo had expressed the desire to talk to Pardo privately. The six friends bade each other good night, and Giuseppe invited Angelo to go upstairs to his study, where they could talk.

Angelo's Questions

Pardo and Angelo reached the study and sat in silence. Angelo could not talk. Pardo said, "First of all, you want to cry." And Angelo started to cry. Giuseppe had understood him; he needed to cry in the presence of someone who would commune with his tears. And he cried, covering his wet face with his hands. Looking at the young man's stooping body, Pardo could not help comparing the way he was now with the way he had been as a student at the University of Pisa, when he had looked forward with vigor and zest to the promise of life.

In the past Pardo had liked to mingle with the students of the university. Before 1938 many Jewish students came to Italian universities from foreign countries, especially from Eastern Europe, because it was difficult or impossible for them to be accepted by universities in their own countries, and especially by medical schools. Some of them came to the University of Pisa, where they were admitted without any restrictions if they had fulfilled the preliminary scholastic requirements. Some were in poor financial condition; some felt rootless and isolated in a country so different from theirs. Pardo had helped many of them to feel at home. In some cases his help was also financial. A few who decided to settle in Italy after they finished their studies were helped by him with professional or business introductions.

Another group of students who maintained social contact with Pardo, the group to which I belonged, consisted of students from Pisa or neighboring towns, especially Leghorn. We did not need financial assistance, nor were we in need of soothing for homesickness. We, too, used to be invited to Pardo's home, and we enjoyed going there. To some of us Pardo was a combination of teacher, uncle, guide, and generous host. At times petty jealousies and feelings of competition developed among us over who was Pardo's favorite. I remember occasionally having pangs of jealousy when I thought Pardo preferred Renzo Toaff, a fellow medical student, to me. Renzo came from a family of rabbis and was much more erudite in Hebrew culture. He is now a leading gynecologist in Israel.

Pardo was at his best among these young people. No trace of his illness remained in him when he was with them. He was no longer the afflicted man, but a much respected person who engaged in debates with the students, both as leader and as peer.

Even when, after graduation, these students moved to other towns or returned to their original countries, some remembered Pardo and kept in touch with him. Angelo Luzzatto was one of these. After his marriage he moved to Parma, but he was always conscious of the important role Pardo had played in his life when he was in his teens and early twenties.

Angelo composed himself after five or ten minutes and said, "I had a presentiment not to leave her alone, but I had a few things to attend to before both of us could leave Parma. We had moved to a part of the city where nobody knew us, and we felt relatively safe. When the neighbor told me what happened, my first impulse was to go to the German headquarters with a gun and kill as many of them as possible. But some inner voice told me, 'This is an insane and useless action. You will not rescue her, and you will cause German retaliation against innocent people. Follow your neighbor's advice. Go away—fast.' Giuseppe, was I right in escaping while she was being deported? Shouldn't I have tried to join her?"

"What you did was right," replied Pardo. "If the Germans had taken you, too, probably they would not have kept you and Bice together. We do not know what happens to people who are deported. Let's hope and pray that Bice will come back safe. What we do know is that Bice is praying that you succeed in saving yourself. I believe she rejoiced in her heart that you were not home when they came."

"I am sure she did. But can *I* accept this situation? What if they kill her?"

Pardo replied, "Isaiah once compared Israel to an olive tree beaten by a storm.[1] Many olives fall and perish, but some remain on the uppermost bough or on the branches. Those few that do not yield to the wind remain on the tree and eventually become new olive trees. If you happen to be among the olives that remain on the tree, don't feel guilty, for your function, too, will be a hard one. From you new trees must germinate, and it is difficult to sprout and grow after a serious storm."

"Giuseppe," said Angelo, "I don't know whether I'm going to be an olive that remains on the tree. I have decided to go over to the Allies' side and fight as one of them. That's why I'm here in Pisa, so I can cross the line."

"How did you arrive at this decision?"

"After what happened to Bice, I tried to join the partisans near Bologna; but they said I was too well known in the north. It would be better if I tried to join the Allies. The partisans said they'd help me do so, near Pisa. I wanted to do what Eugenio Calò did. Since they took his wife, he has fought the Germans at times with the partisans, at times with the Allies. He has crossed the line many

1. Isaiah, 17:6.

times.[2] I don't have in me the capacity to equal him, but I shall do my best to follow his example."

Angelo continued, "I believe, Giuseppe, that if we have to meet death, the best way is in fighting the oppressor. Why do many of us Jews let ourselves be captured, one by one, without any resistance?"

"Many Jews fight the oppressor with arms, as Eugenio does, and as you intend to do. They organize resistance wherever they have sufficient numbers, as they did last year in the Warsaw ghetto, where each one of them met death. As servants of God, most Jews will fight evil in whatever way they can."

"Servants of God! Hollow words, Giuseppe. They remind me of my childhood, when I was a boy in Sunday school. That was a millennium ago, when there was no hint of what was to come. I am totally confused, and I feel endlessly melancholy. I distrust every human being, even myself. Is it worthwhile to cross the line? Is any cause worthwhile? Can you give me an answer? I thought you were the only one who could, and that's why I rang your bell."

Pardo understood that Angelo's melancholy was full of anger, the chained force of a youth full of desires. He said, "I'll listen to you, and I'll try to help you. But it's dangerous for you to stay here. I want you to know that."

"I cannot meet my contact before 10:00 P.M. We're to meet near Santa Caterina Church, and the risk isn't any greater here than in streets patrolled by military police. I do have a false curfew permit, but I don't want to have to use it." A curfew permit enabled people with special duties, like doctors and nurses, to

---

2. After the loss of his family, Eugenio Calò organized partisan groups of resistance against the Germans. Captured several times, he always succeeded in escaping. He was eventually captured and tortured for the purpose of making him reveal the names of other partisans and partisan organizations. He maintained his silence. He was buried up to his neck, together with several others. Finally the Germans lit a fuse that detonated the dynamite that killed all of them. Calò was posthumously given the gold medal for military heroism.

leave their homes at any time. During the summer of 1944 in the part of Pisa occupied by the Germans, people without that permit could leave their homes only from 10:00 A.M. to 12:00 noon.

"If something should happen," Pardo said, "or if we hear a suspicious noise before it's time for you to go, run out to the garden. Jump over the wall into the backyard of the next house. Nobody lives there now. I'll see to it that tomorrow morning somebody from the Palagini family comes to help you. They are Christian neighbors, friends, and tenants of mine who live in the house next to the one that is empty."

"Giuseppe, sometimes it seems to me that I have become as insensitive as a stone. Other times, like now, I'm so full of feeling that I wish I could scream or cry without stopping. I feel I am trapped in an absurd world. Are we all? Do you feel that way, too? I feel betrayed and cheated by everybody. Where is my brother? Perhaps only you are my teacher and my brother, but only if you can help me understand.

"You know, my father raised me to be patriotic. Our ancestors have been in this country for many centuries. Italy is my love. When this anti-Semitism started, I found myself in exile, living in ways I could never have predicted. But since the war started, I no longer feel in exile in an outlandish country. I find myself in enemy territory, surrounded by constant present dangers. Death is likely to be around the corner. I may leave this home, disregarding the curfew, and somebody lying in wait may shoot me.

"Giuseppe, why this wide conspiracy against us, a tiny, inconspicuous segment of humanity? Have we in any way contributed to this? Do we deserve it?"

Pardo replied, "Angelo, read the Book of Job again. You speak like Job's friends. What happens to us is not necessarily what we deserve.

"Remember also that before they rejected us Jews, the Nazi rulers rejected their own; they rejected what Bach, Kant, and Goethe stood for. They have masked a pattern of evil as a pattern of duty, and slavery to their government as the highest freedom of the spirit. They have taught that what ought to be, ought not to be. They hate love and love hate. Where freedom is denied, not only do we Jews feel in exile, but Christians also.

"But for us, as you said, it is worse. We are few, yes, but not inconspicuous, and we have been highly vocal in letting people know what we stand for. We have learned from Isaiah to hope for the day when people beat their swords into plowshares and their spears into pruninghooks.[3] What does Hitler write in the very first page of *Mein Kampf*? The Nazis must beat their plows and pruninghooks into swords and spears. This reversal of the biblical sentence at the start of that book of hate tells the whole story.

"The New Testament, too, stands for abolition of war and hate, and for universal love, but in his ideology Hitler is not any less anti-Christian than anti-Jewish, and as deaf to the message of Jesus and Francis of Assisi as to that of Moses and Isaiah. But he needs the Christians as instruments of power; the Jews he needs as targets of his hate. We make the best possible scapegoat. We are few, spread out all over, and defenseless. We have been the object of historical prejudice, and we have always openly opposed tyrannies of all kinds, whether right or left. Since we were in Egypt, over three thousand years ago, we have been intolerant of persecution and all insults to human dignity, and each year at Passover we celebrate freedom. We easily protest. The Bible says we have a stiff neck that does not easily bend."

"Giuseppe, can you get at my personal sorrow? Can you speak about the ideals I grew up with, the pillars of my existence, which are now crumbling? I feel I must ask you three questions. I hope you will answer them. Please try; then I'll go.

"The first seems unimportant, and people who are not Italian would even consider it ludicrous. During the First World War my patriotic father enlisted in the army, although he was too old for

3. Isaiah 2:4.

conscription. He was loyal to the House of Savoy, and he brought me up the same way. He used to say that any form of government, like Fascism, comes and goes, but the king stays. The king is above everything, the protector of all Italians, including the minorities. On ascending the throne, the king swore allegiance to a liberal constitution. I accepted my father's belief and defended the king on many occasions. And then I had to admit that he did not stop Mussolini from abrogating civil rights, from waging immoral wars, from persecuting innocent people. He put his royal seal on every act of the Fascist regime. The person my father trusted so much became the accomplice of the murderers of Matteotti and of the Rosselli brothers. This king opened up a series of events, a chain of crimes, leading to the capturing of my Bice, my poor Bice."

After Angelo composed himself, Pardo replied, "Many well-intentioned people felt like your father. They were misled by tradition and the falsification of history. Your father's error, and that of many other people, was the belief that an institution like the monarchy is modeled after the institutions of Heaven. But the monarchy has nothing heavenly in its making, and its only aim is the preservation of political power. The king of Italy was the person who, more easily than anyone else, could have stopped Mussolini, but he did not lift a finger until he himself was in danger, with the Allies already on Italian soil. For the plight of us Italian Jews the king is no less accountable than Mussolini."

Pardo and Angelo were absorbed in their reflections about Mussolini and the treacherous king when they heard a sudden noise. Angelo leaped up, ready to run to the garden, jump over the wall, and find refuge in the abandoned house, as Pardo had instructed him. Pardo too rose, alarmed. But the noise became more distinct and was soon recognized as the weeping of a young girl, perhaps in her middle teens or slightly older. The crying was from the neighbors' apartment next door.

Noises of planes, cannons, bombs, and machine guns often

drown out all the little sounds of normal living in time of war. But there are also stretches of absolute silence that seem interminable until they are interrupted. Small and isolated noises then become unusually audible, capable even of breaching thick walls. At such times, also, every noise is presumed ominous until proved otherwise.

The weeping of the girl continued, interrupted by some indistinct words of an older woman. Was the girl's pain part of the great pain? Did she mourn for a dear one, a father, a brother, slain in the war? Giuseppe and Angelo put their heads close to the wall and tried to listen. They did not think this was an invasion of privacy. Whatever affects people in time of war moves into the public domain.

The girl was sobbing, and the voice of the older woman was intermittently strident. The crying seemed rhythmic and sweet, like a song. The speech of the woman was not harsh, but somewhat hoarse and abrupt. The crying was poetry, the talking prose. What was the matter?

At this point the door of the study opened. Silvia came in. "Excuse me, Signor Pardo," she said, "I heard the noise, and I wanted to reassure you. I know this din from next door very well. The woman, Clotilde, does not leave her daughter in peace. She does not want Annina to be in love with Gino, a shoemaker's son." Now Angelo and Pardo could hear, clearly distinguishable, the voice of Clotilde. "You must not see him any more . . . no more . . . no more."

And the girl, too, was heard again, sobbing and crying, but the crying soon faded away, probably because she had moved away to another room. Silvia said, "Clotilde has no right to do that to the girl." Angelo and Pardo looked at Silvia. There was sorrow in her face and sadness in her voice at the thought of poor Annina. Angelo and Pardo smiled at each other. While millions had been killed and more would die, the love lament of an adolescent girl had risen tenderly in the calm of the evening. For Giuseppe and

Angelo the girl's lament was a hymn to the right to love at the time of the greatest hate.

As Silvia was leaving the room, Giuseppe and Angelo both looked with affection at the woman who insisted on continuing to work in that house, at the risk of her life. They also looked at each other, and each of them understood what the other was thinking. Why could Silvia so easily separate Annina's sorrow from the huge disaster and respond so tenderly? Because for Silvia, each of them thought, Annina's sorrow was a sorrow, as an olive lost in a storm is still to be regretted as an olive lost.

Angelo made an effort to proceed to his second question. "Giuseppe, I am not a Catholic, but since I was raised in a Catholic country, I learned to respect the pope. I thought that as spiritual leader of the largest Christian group he was a guardian of all people. For over five years I have expected him to intervene in our favor. Giuseppe, how can it be that Pius XII has remained silent about the persecution of the Jews?"

"Let me remind you, Angelo, that the previous pope, Pius XI, was very much against racial hate. The next pope may be one who will promote love and understanding among all faiths. Perhaps you remember that on February 10, 1939, Pius XI suddenly died. Well, on the very next day, February 11, which was the tenth anniversary of the end of the historic dispute between the Catholic Church and the Italian government, Pius XI had been scheduled to make a speech condemning totalitarianism and racial persecution. His words were never heard. Why his successor has never spoken in defense of the Jews I cannot tell you. I don't even have a hypothesis. But this is not a Jewish problem even if Jews are the sufferers; it is a Christian problem. It will be up to the Christians of the future to search for and find explanations."

"Did any other pope in the past dare to defend the Jews in similar circumstances?"

"Some. There was Clement VI."

"When was he pope?"

"Toward the middle of the fourteenth century. It is easy for us Pisans to remember, because he is the pope who, in 1343, with a papal bull, legitimatized the founding of our university. Then between 1347 and 1354 came the plague, which killed off millions all over Europe. The rumor began to be spread that the Jews were responsible. The leaders did nothing to discourage this rumor because it was so useful to them that the populace had found a culprit to hold responsible for their sufferings, and a scapegoat. In Germany alone, 350 Jewish communities were exterminated; the rest moved to Eastern Europe. But Pope Clement VI raised his voice and said, 'Christians, stop. Jews are just as much the victims of the plague as you are, and not the cause.'"

Angelo replied, "Even in the darkest ages there were people who defended us, but not in this twentieth century. We have been totally abandoned. And that leads to my next question—the most difficult, and the one I was really coming to, because it is the one about which I care infinitely more than the first two." Angelo's voice trembled and his face was contorted, as if what he was about to say required the greatest effort. "I can understand the callousness of a king, and even the silence of a pope, who is a human being, but what about the silence of God? Why is He mute? Why does He permit these things to happen? Why is He absent when His presence is so terribly needed?"

Pardo, a devout man, was taken aback, shocked; his face was pale and full of pain. Angelo looked at him intently; he had seen the face of the parnas looking like that once before. When? Oh, yes, he remembered it was on a Saturday morning, many years before. Pardo had been walking home from the synagogue. A group of adolescents were waiting in ambush for him. They had a dog. The boys knew that Pardo would be turning from Palestro Street into Sant' Andrea Street. As Pardo reached the corner, the boys released the dog, pushing it toward him. The dog was barking and the boys were adding to the uproar by loudly imitating dogs barking.

Angelo was at that moment on the other side of the street, but Pardo had not seen him. Angelo did not know what to do. His first impulse was to rush toward the boys and disperse them. But he stopped. Would Pardo feel that being caught by Angelo in such a situation was a worse humiliation than being ridiculed by these urchins? Angelo decided that Pardo would be able to handle the situation by himself. And so he did. He maintained his composure and continued to walk straight along Sant' Andrea Street. But his face was stiffened by panic and had a terrible pallor.

Now Angelo wondered if he had unintentionally caused a similar terror in Pardo. What would Pardo do?

Pardo composed himself again and said with vigor, "God is not mute! Each crime bespeaks His lament, 'How far you are from Me!' The greater the crime, the greater is God's reminder of how much is within the realm of man's choice and grasp. But we must choose to hear Him. We do not hear. People still prefer swords and spears. The era Isaiah foresaw is not yet here, and the whole world is still in exile. Perhaps the greater the suffering, the sooner people will reject evil and hasten the end of the exile."

"Then you feel that we should not fight evil but make it run its course, because ultimately its effect will be good?"

"No, we must fight evil in any possible way. Evil, too, may be a servant of God, but only if it is fought and in this way brings about goodness."

"Giuseppe, you talk about the voice of God as if He spoke through people's evil, as if His goodness would eventually reveal itself as a result of this evil. Where is the direct voice of goodness? Where is the direct voice of God? Why don't I hear it?"

"God's voice of goodness is spoken through intermediaries only. Many people bring His message, everywhere, in this home, too, at this very moment. Think of Silvia, and of Giovanna and Alice. Why do they stay here? Why can't I convince these three Christian women to quit? Because I pay them? Because I hypnotize them? Because they are in awe of me, as my guests are? I'll tell you why. They follow a voice that comes from the heart—and makes them risk everything. It is the voice of God, and we hear it, too, through them. These women know that without them we bewildered old people would be lost. Silvia is my Christian guardian; she, not the pope. These three Christian women undo Hitler, Mussolini, and the king for me."

"Yes, yes," said Angelo, warming. "Yes, and there are many others like them all over the world. One is the neighbor in Parma who warned me."

"These people are suffering, too," said Pardo. "For many the countries in which they live are gigantic jails with invisible bars where one cannot say what one thinks, or act as one wants, or leave if one wishes to. The smaller jails, those with real bars where official prisoners are detained and tortured, are the most visible. But under tyranny hundreds of millions of men and women daily undergo spiritual death. We Jews are being put into visible jails, into concentration camps, and in large numbers we are being put to physical death. We make visible what may otherwise remain invisible. We are the red flags, the sentinels; we make the world hear the suffering that the majority endures silently, and the lament that most non-Jews only whisper. Perhaps that is our fate."

"Our fate? But if it is fate, we have nothing to do with choosing our life."

"Even if fate exists, and I am not sure it does, it becomes one's inward necessity. That's what counts."

"Giuseppe, I am not sure I understand you. You see the possibility of a good end in everything. I hope I come to accept your ideas. But tell me, if these things we hear are true, if all the people who are deported are exterminated, how can this catastrophe bring goodness? Wouldn't a cloud of darkness always surround the earth, even if only as a memory of what happened in our time? Wouldn't astronomers from other solar systems call this the infamous planet?"

"Certainly if we are in the middle of a huge massacre, then a new era must be starting in the world. The confrontation between good and evil is eternal, but only now we may have come to know the full potentiality of evil. And perhaps before the war is over, other events may show that such potentiality is so great as to destroy not God's cosmos but the family of man, this family that chose evil although it knew the warmth of love and the light of goodness. But I cannot believe that the forces of dissolution will prevail forever. The love I have for people like you and for what God has created makes it impossible for me to accept an ultimate futility in everything. To believe in nothingness is worse than to believe in power, is more tragic than Hitler."

Pardo paused for a while; then he added softly, "Angelo, let hope grow in your heart, like roses in a garden; don't leave room only for the weeds of despair. If a holocaust is taking place now, I believe it is the decisive event that divides time into a period in which man did not know total evil and one in which he learned to know it. Such knowledge is like that acquired by the first couple on earth, according to Genesis."

"How will new generations react to this knowledge?"

"I am not a prophet. I can only guess and hope. I believe that in the beginning they will not comprehend the significance of the event. Some will understand but will try to suppress the memory of it because of shame, guilt, or indifference. Then people will begin to understand in a confused way. For some time the impact will not be pleasant. The new generation will distrust what the older generation abided by. They will believe only in what is available now and in what offers immediate satisfaction. They will not recoil from any sensation and will be driven by an insatiable hunger. But I believe that eventually people will recognize that they cannot be satisfied as long as they do not search for the right food. They will come to know that their hunger is for broader horizons and for eternal values. They will return. The ascent to goodness will resume its course.

"In the past, historical regressions have not prevented man from resuming his quest for the beyond. Perhaps in an order that embraces the cosmos, the present era is needed to give people new vistas and new vigor in their upward journey. Fifty years from now the world will be fifty years closer to the end of the exile. Fifty years from now people may again love love, without holding in hatred those who chose hate in our time, because that hate eventually led to a longing for a greater love. We must love one another more after what we have discovered during this war. Whoever ignores the holocaust will continue to see history with old eyes and will not grasp the new potentiality for goodness."

Angelo was moved by Giuseppe but not yet satisfied. He was trying to take in everything the parnas had said, but he couldn't. He had come to Pardo's home to make his older friend aware of the fullness of the evil that was upon them. Instead, he had found himself strangely being kindled with a new kind of hope. He felt himself no longer the same man, even if he had not completely understood what he heard.

He said, "Giuseppe, I must leave now, before I fully understand what you are saying. Maybe in the next few days, if I have time to consider what you told me, everything will be clearer. One thing I do know: I was fortunate to see you again. At least this was given to me, to see you again, and to hear of love and hope in a day darkened by despair. At least I know that *you* I can still trust, as I did then, when I was a boy. You told me what you believe in, frankly and with love. More I could not ask."

A knocking at the door. From the gentleness of the sound, Giuseppe knew who was there. "Ernesto," he said. The door opened, and it was Ernesto. With a gentle smile he said, "Excuse me for intruding, but I did not hear Angelo leave when he was supposed to. I wondered if anything had happened."

"Nothing alarming," said Angelo. "Giuseppe helped me overcome some doubts, but I still have a great deal of thinking to do. Giuseppe tried to restore what was once my basic optimism, my belief in a friendly universe."

"Don't misunderstand me, Angelo," said Pardo. "During my

adolescence I stopped believing in a friendly universe. What I believe now is that we must make it friendly."

"Yes, we must. Even if we have to fight and kill and die. But before I leave, Giuseppe, let me ask you for the last time, why don't you leave this dangerous place?"

"Please, don't ask. I have decided to stay," said Pardo.

"And you, Signor Ernesto, why don't you and the other guests leave at once?"

"Please, don't ask. We have decided to stay," said Ernesto.

Angelo knew there was no point in pursuing the matter. He told them hurriedly what he was going to do. He would go to St. Caterina's Church, which was not far from Pardo's house. A man coming in from the village of Vecchiano would meet him there and accompany him through the pinewood that stretches from San Rossore to Migliarino. They would go by bicycle on paths in the woods familiar to his guide. Somewhat north of the mouth of the Serchio River another man with a sailboat would be waiting for him, and Angelo would attempt to cross the line by sea in this sailboat. If the wind blew the wrong way, Angelo would go to Corsica, south of Bastia. There he knew how to get in touch with people from the underground who would hide him in the mountains in the central part of the island. He had food and money in his sack and did not need anything. He was not carrying anything that would betray his identity.

"Good luck," said Ernesto, shaking hands with Angelo.

"Good luck," said Giuseppe. "The wind be with you."

Giuseppe and Angelo wanted to embrace, but instead they looked intently at each other, trying to derive from the look a presentiment, a sign that would indicate whether or not they would see each other again. No such clue appeared. All that emerged was what they felt for one another.

Pardo and Ernesto

From a window slightly ajar, Pardo and Ernesto watched Angelo rapidly disappearing into the darkness of Sant' Andrea Street.

Ernesto was about to leave when Pardo said, "Please stay for a while if you are not too tired. I'd like to talk to you."

"Of course. Cesira is already asleep. She won't even know I'm not there."

"Ernesto, you were the first one to use that word, Shekhinah, this afternoon. Therefore I must talk to you and convince you of how sick a man I am."

"Giuseppe, I shall listen to you as a person who cares for you very much. But speak to me only if you feel like talking, if talking will make you feel better."

"I have no wine or liquor to offer you, only the light of this kerosene lamp, for as long as it lasts. I sense the urgency of solving in a day or two what I have not been able to clarify in a lifetime. I must also understand why I don't leave this place and why I don't request more strongly that all of you leave. Am I more afraid of my illness than of the Nazis? Is that all there is in this matter, and no more? Had I not been ill, probably I would have left. I have tried to convince all of you to leave, but you refused to do so. I have seen how the group responded to Angelo's arrival.

He came and brought us much bad news. But what he told us did not make you change your minds. On the contrary, it reinforced your belief that since nothing has happened to us so far this is a safe place; and my illness, too, becomes a protection. Couldn't it be that my illness makes me a great coward?"

"Giuseppe," replied Ernesto, "the things you have done in life bespeak courage, not cowardice."

"I want to tell you more about my illness. And yet it is hard for me to open up this matter even to friends, lest I appear to them as I appear to myself—crazy. And if I am crazy, did I have the right to be the president of the Jewish congregation of Pisa? But you did not belong to the congregation; you are not a Pisan. You may be more lenient."

"I have known many Pisan Jews, and I know that each of them has the greatest admiration for you. If you have made errors, they have to be attributed to the fact that you are human, not to your illness. The congregation has always had a strong affection for you."

"And I for them. Oh, Ernesto! Let me talk first about this little congregation. I like to brag about it to you, a man from another city. I want to talk about them all and mention their names, most of which will probably mean nothing to you. But please indulge me; I shall try not to abuse your patience."

"Of course, Giuseppe. This is your family, and you are proud of it."

"Like a grandfather who at the end of his life makes a mental survey of his kin . . ."

"Like a patriarch."

". . . and this grandfather sees that by and large his people have made good use of their lives. This congregation has always been very small, but even recently it had glorious days, Ernesto. We had a distinguished senator among us, David Supino, and famous literati like Alessandro D'Ancona, and a poet, Ugo Ghiron. The Pontecorvo family built one of the largest textile factories in the country here, and businessmen, especially in the textile trade, have made the city prosperous. Each member stands out in my mind and is dear to me: Signora Luisa Orvieto, the grammar school teacher of our parochial school, who has educated many generations of children, and her husband, Felice, a little, short man, a pillar of the synagogue. And Vittoria and Elda Millul, two sisters who never married and dedicated themselves to teaching in our Sunday school. There is Giacomo Bemporad, a generous man who came here from Piedmont as a peddler and built a chain of prosperous stores, and Arturo Bolaffi, a silk merchant who kept his store closed every Saturday in spite of the city's disapproval. And many professors of the university, and many others whose names may be totally unknown to you: De Cori, Ventura, Sadun, Nissim, Pirani, Arieti, Franco, Samaia, Lascar, and Naftoli Emdin, who came from distant Russia. I have not yet even mentioned our rabbi, Augusto Hasdà, a good-hearted and straightforward man. He and I have had our disagreements, but we worked them out. He has left; I do not know what has happened to him." [1]

Pardo went on, "I have bored you with a list of names you cannot possibly remember. Forgive me, Ernesto. But I have discovered something while I was mentioning these people's names. It was as if I were asking each of them, 'Would you have chosen me as your parnas if you knew the extent of my illness?' I cannot ask them; I ask you, who are not a Pisan and have nothing to do with my appointment. You are the judge now, and for another and most important reason. You must decide whether it is my illness that prevents all of you from leaving. It is not too late for you to go. Even at this hour you may convince the others to go."

"Giuseppe, when you spoke about the members of your congregation, you made me envious of them. I hope to become one of them soon."

1. On November 29, 1943, while away from Pisa, the rabbi and his wife Bettina were captured by the Nazis and sent to an extermination camp, from which they never returned.

"I don't speak about my illness even to Dario, who is my doctor. But I must talk to you now, without any further delay.

"I am constantly in a state of expectation that animals will come after me, jump on me, bite me, torture me, or even kill me. I am afraid of all animals—lions, tigers, and snakes. But of course I know there are no lions or tigers in Pisa; thus my fears, or phobias, as the doctors call them, center on animals that I can see, like horses, cats, and particularly dogs, especially those that remind me of wolves.

"Why do I expect these animals to attack me? I am completely in the dark. Occasionally I am also afraid that they might invade my house, but if I go out, my fears are worse. Until a few months ago I could overcome the fear with strenuous effort. Now the idea of going far away from home, to another city, or to the country, increases my anxiety to the point of panic. I know that these fears are absurd to the point of being ridiculous, but it is useless to tell myself so. I cannot overcome them.

"You see, at times I have seen animals and a terror has taken hold of me. Its intensity is just as great as its absurdity. I am lost. My heart beats fast; my face no doubt changes expression. I am no longer myself. The panic increases, and the fear of the fear increases the fear. A crescendo of suffering engulfs me. I believe I will not be able to hold my own. I search for help; I don't know where to find it. I am ashamed to ask for help, and yet I am afraid the fear will make me die. I do die, like a coward, a thousand deaths. But then courage returns. I do not die; I survive, only to face more and more fears. When I am not exposed to animals, I am afraid that the animals will, strangely, appear. It is especially at night, when I am about to go to bed, that I expect to see them, maybe because I am tired, maybe because the problems of the day reappear all at once.

"At times the phobias are more than phobias. I fancy that I hear animals; any noise suggests the possible presence of one. Sometimes I hear the distant barking of a dog—I suppose the dog of a neighbor—and the barking sounds to me like the howling of a wolf. When I hear animals barking, neighing, braying, I expect them to jump at me. Occasionally these phobias have driven me to do regrettable things. For instance, once I evicted a family of friends from one of the houses I own, across the street from my own house, because they had bought a dog. I found a silly excuse to evict them. It spoiled the friendship for a while, but then we became friends again. Of course, they could not know why I evicted them. On the whole, however, my illness has not caused me serious trouble with other people."

At this point a loud noise was heard, again from the next house. This time it was not the sound of crying, but an uncontrollable and prolonged laughter.

"They heard us," said Pardo, alarmed. "Do you see? They are laughing at me." The laughing continued, completely blotting out the voices of the people.

"No," said Ernesto. "They cannot hear us; they cannot make out our words."

"But," Pardo replied, "people have often laughed at me, and you know it. What could they be laughing about in such a way if not at me? These are not times when people laugh."

Ernesto was taken aback, not knowing what to say; yet he was sure that if Giuseppe were not so preoccupied with his illness, he would not think that the laughter had anything to do with him.

He replied, "These are times when people cry. But there are a few people who are able to laugh at all this, to laugh off world's affairs. They think the trouble is so big that we can do nothing about it; we can only laugh at it. Mightn't your neighbor be one of those who are able to laugh off this nonsensical war, this stupid game?"

Pardo replied, "I was wrong, of course. They could not hear our words; even if they could, they would not laugh at me." He paused briefly, then added, "I don't believe you are right, though. My neighbor is not a Greek god on Olympus, making fun of little scatterbrained men fidgeting and playing with death."

A knock at the door. Pardo, again recognizing the gentleness of the knocking, said, "Silvia?" The door opened, and it was Silvia.

"Oh," said Pardo to Silvia, "you heard the noise and came to reassure me. Silvia, we do not let you sleep tonight."

There were signs of weariness on Silvia's face. Her eyes were darkly circled, but not so much that she could not brighten them with a smile.

"I was about to finish in the kitchen," she said. "This Signor Torquato—when he laughs, he laughs. You can hear him a mile away. And he makes everybody laugh." Silvia started to chuckle, too, as if carried away by the scene she was visualizing in the adjacent apartment.

"Thank you, Silvia," Pardo and Ernesto said as she was leaving, and they looked at each other with amazement. What was obvious to Silvia had been so difficult for them to recognize, that for most folk of the world good laughter was good laughter, even in terrible times.

Pardo said, "Signor Torquato reminds us that tomorrow morning the sun will rise again. The war does not stop the earth from rotating on its axis."

Ernesto continued, "Giuseppe, since you want to talk about your illness, let me ask a question. You must have consulted some doctors. What did they say?"

"The doctors don't know much about this condition, even though they have known of its existence for a long time. Hippocrates was the first one to describe it, over two thousand years ago. Psychiatry is not very advanced, at least in Italy. A few doctors gave me some tonics and sedatives—a complete waste of time. Some spoke of degeneration of the central nervous system, for which there is no remedy. I myself have read the literature and become quite competent on this subject from a theoretical point of view. I have read what Stanley Hall and Pierre Janet have written about it, but with no benefit whatsoever."

"I have heard that psychoanalysts especially have studied your condition. Have you consulted any of them?"

"I consulted a psychoanalyst from Vienna, a pupil of Freud's, who said that the animals I am afraid of stand for my father. According to him I am still waiting for punishment from my father. But I have no recollection whatsoever of ever having hated my father, or of having been so afraid of him. I doubt that these feelings are still in my unconscious. The whole interpretation does not make any sense to me."

"It does not make sense to me, either. But how did psychoanalysts reach this conclusion? Do you know?"

"I told you that I have become an expert on phobias, as expert as a layman can be. Are you really interested?"

"There's a pretty good quantity of kerosene left in the lamp, and you promised to talk as long as it lasted."

"Well, before Freud, nobody tried to give a special meaning to phobias; they were just considered symptoms that a disordered mind produced. Many people still think so today. Freud happened to study this illness in a five-year-old boy, Hans, who had developed the fear that a horse would bite him. Freud explained that horses really had nothing to do with Hans's fear. The boy was afraid of being punished by his father, and in his unconscious mind the horse had become a symbol of his father."

"But why should Hans be so afraid of his father?"

"He had what Freud called an Oedipus complex—a strong desire for the woman with whom he was in close contact, his mother—and he developed a hatred for his father, whom he saw as his rival."

"All this is quite difficult for me to grasp. How do horses enter the picture?"

"Hans also had feelings of love for his father. But how can a little child love and hate his own father at the same time? How can he live with a parent by whom he expects at any time to be severely punished? According to Freud, Hans's mind built a curtain that covered up what made the child unhappy and confused. Hans became completely unaware of the sexual desire for his mother and the fear of his father, but the fear was replaced by another fear, the fear of horses. The horse stood for his father. Hans could go on loving his father by being concerned only with the problem of avoiding horses. He could more easily avoid the sight of horses, although they were very common in Vienna at that time, than the sight of his father."

"What has all this to do with you?"

"I don't know. My belief is that it has nothing to do with me. Perhaps I think this way because I never underwent psychoanalytic treatment and never discovered what is in my unconscious mind. On the other hand, I know that psychoanalysts have not confirmed the connection between phobias and sexual desires that occur in childhood. I remember my childhood fairly well. Earlier tonight, when Angelo was leaving and mentioned the basic optimism he used to have, the belief in a friendly universe, I answered . . ."

"I remember. You answered that you, too, used to believe in a friendly world until a change occurred in your adolescence."

"That's right. There was an optimism in my childhood that came from having a home blessed by affection and without want. My mother and father were there to offer love, affection, warmth, everything I needed. Life was good and there to be enjoyed. Then something happened."

"What happened?"

"I gradually woke up, as from a dream. I no longer saw life as beautiful. I became aware of the precarious state of all existence, including my own. I discovered danger, the danger that is everywhere and around all of us. I became aware that the universe can be very unfriendly. It was too serious a crisis for me to bear at such a young age. I did not know what to do. Then finally the answer came to me, the one I told Angelo. The world is not friendly. *We have to make it friendly;* it is up to us. It was in part up to me."

"Giuseppe, now that you have started, perhaps you can tell me more. Perhaps together we can find a little understanding. How did it come to be that you felt the universe was unfriendly?"

"I do not know. It was as if a large veil had been covering the world before. My supposition is that I was more interested in the veil than in the world. The veil was woven with the love and softness of my mother, the warm concern and sober advice of my father, the friendship of the little Jewish congregation, the reassurance and faith of the Torah, the beauty of Pisa, the peace of this quiet Sant' Andrea Street, the serenity of my home and garden.

"In my adolescence I was given to philosophical speculation beyond my grasp and knowledge. I became involved with the problem of evil. I started to read how Jews had been massacred by the Crusaders in the Middle Ages, but I could not continue. It was too painful. I even started to dismiss what I read as untrue. I could not believe that people engaged in what they considered a sacred mission could indulge in such barbaric acts. Then I became involved in studying the period of the Black Plague, and again I could not believe that innocent people could be blamed and destroyed. I started to study the Spanish Inquisition and what happened to our ancestors before they came here to Italy. I refused to believe. I remember asking myself, 'How can this be true?' but I found no answer.

"One day in high school the Latin teacher was making us translate the Latin proverb *Homo homini lupus*, and in a stubborn way I said to myself, 'This proverb is false. Man does not act like a wolf to a man.' I refused to accept that concept. And then— Ernesto, I do remember now what happened. I instantly became afraid of wolves. Freud is right. I did what he explained so well; I displaced. I became afraid of wolves, and then of dogs, which resemble wolves, and then of all animals."

"Giuseppe," said Ernesto, with vigor, "I believe you are close to the truth."

"But why did I do that?"

"Because you wanted to remain a friend of man. You wanted to make the world friendly. I am a layman; I cannot be sure about these things, but I think that for a sensitive personality like yours it was unacceptable that a man can be a wolf to another man. I think Freud is right. You did what little Hans did. You accepted that only a wild beast like a wolf can be an enemy of a human being. You had to become neurotic in order to undo what you came to learn in your studies, in order to refuse to believe that what you saw around you as an adolescent was so different from the little, honest, and safe world of your childhood. At the price of becoming ill, you tried to save the image of man.

"I was right this afternoon when I said that your illness is part of the Shekhinah with which you are touched. What is ill in you is intertwined with what is strong and holy and springs from the same source. Your illness is demanded of you."

"Your words touch me deeply," said Giuseppe. "What you say makes sense. Perhaps this strange night, and your friendship, and your uncommon words, make your interpretation seem plausible to me. Nevertheless, what we are considering remains only a hypothesis. I cannot be sure. I shall think about it. A wolf is a wolf for me, and a man is a man. I need some kind of proof, but I don't know from where it could come.

"I do agree that my illness has a meaning. What has to such a large extent shaped my life cannot be just an aberration of my mind. It must have a meaning, at least for me, the prisoner and the bearer of this affliction. Therefore I should not try to escape from it but do what it requires me to do, even to stay here at this time. I must consider my illness as something I must hold on to, observe, and even respect, until the time comes when I can understand it fully or be sure of its meaning.

"I know that I could follow the instinct of preservation and try to escape to safety. I could be guided by what Angelo, our times, and history tell us to do and leave at once. But I will be guided by what I feel I should do. Up to the last breath I shall try to discover the secret of my illness, of my life. This search is my life's adventure."

After a pause, he continued. "What I am trying to say to you, Ernesto, is that my illness is more than an illness to me, but not to you, not to my other guests. You do not need to stay. Run away, this very night. Now. You may still have time to escape. Wake them up. Go."

"If your illness is more than an illness for you, it is more than an illness for us, too, Giuseppe. We, your guests, have already found a meaning in your illness. It may be different from the one you search for, but it is enough for us, enough to make us decide to stay. Your illness is for us part of the Shekhinah that has come to rest upon you. You say that you must become sure of your illness's meaning by staying here; we shall support you in this adventure of your life."

Pardo said, "We have suggested that the meaning we search for has to do with evil, not the evil that may inadvertently have occurred in my family, or that was connected with jealousy for my father, but one that loomed in my immature eyes in vaster dimensions when as an adolescent I recognized the existence of evil. Couldn't we believe that mentally ill people like me are more sensitive to what hurts and therefore expect danger and evil more than others? The prophets were sensitive to evil and could bring their message to the people. We mentally ill cannot. Our secret is for others to discover and reveal. My illness, my oppressor, is still inside of me. Oh, I pray God to help me in my endeavor! Oh God, make me discover the secret before I die. Then, when my final hour arrives, I will depart thinking that my life was rightly spent and that I deserved to be the parnas of Pisa.

"I do love this big family of mine, this little congregation of senators and poets, of doctors and professors, of laborers and peddlers."

He paused as if suddenly absorbed by other thoughts; then he continued. "Now practically all the Jews of Pisa have left, and the synagogue is deserted. Whatever Jew is still in Pisa is in this home, and in Pisa this home is the only bearer of the Torah. But some will return; some olives will remain on the branches of the ancient tree." Pardo did not know that there was another Jew hiding in Pisa, Manlio Lascar, about whom we shall learn more later.

"Giuseppe," added Ernesto, "you often mention our prophets. You live according to the way they showed us. They did not escape confrontation with evil, even when they knew evil would triumph. Like them, you know that the triumph of evil is temporary. But it seems to me that in comparison to other people you are involved in a double confrontation. Fascism is the evil that makes us unfree; you have to contend also with an inner problem. You face both adversities with fortitude."

Pardo said, "The lack of freedom caused by an illness stems from the limitations of the human state and is to be overcome eventually by science. The lack of freedom imposed by others comes from the free will of man and indicates man's limitless capacity to choose evil."

"Giuseppe, the kerosene is nearly gone. I would like to ask you one last question. You speak about your illness as a lack of freedom and an impairment of the will, and yet you seem to me a giant of the will, willing to face any kind of adversity. How is this to be reconciled?"

Pardo replied, "My will is unfree as far as my symptoms are concerned. To the extent that my will is unfree, I am unknown to myself and others."

Ernesto said, "Again, Giuseppe, I must tell you again that you face both adversities with fortitude."

"Ernesto, more than one adversity and two types of tragedy frequently visit the human being. In one type, destiny and evil submerge the victim entirely. This is what I call the tragic tragedy. But a tragedy is not tragic, or only apparently so, if through the course of the sad events, it leads to a rise of the spirit—like the tragedy of having to sacrifice one's own beloved son Isaac, the tragedy of Joseph sold as a slave by his own brothers, the tragedy of Job."

Ernesto replied, "With my limited vision I sense I can vouch for this to you, Giuseppe. If your life ends in a tragedy, it will not be the tragic one." Ernesto was infused with the fervor of the moment and felt possessed by an emerging eloquence never before known to him. Though his body was trembling, he said with a steady, firm voice, "The kerosene is almost used up, but I cannot wait til tomorrow; I must say this to you now. The Pisan Jews did *right* in appointing you their parnas. A little ridge separates sanity from the illness of the mind. The Pisan Jews did not allow that little ridge to blur the basic values. They knew that a man's worth is not to be measured by his sanity or insanity, but by the way he faces evil.

"Wise Jews of Pisa! If your story ever comes to be known, perhaps even when the leaning tower that has made this city famous no longer leans, there will be somebody among the children of Israel, or among the people of other faiths, who will think of Pisa because of its parnas. That parnas will tower like a tower that a whimsical imperfection made to lean but not to fall.

"As for us, your guests, what you are still debating within yourself has become a source of certitude and strength; and whatever your uncertain fate will be, it will be our certain fate."

The two looked at each other intensely, while the lamp shed its last light. A silent embrace followed, which included many things for which there was no sure answer, and many others for which there were only eternal answers.

The Guests and
Silvia, Giovanna, and Alice
During the Night of July 31

Ernesto was the last of the guests to retire; the first to reach their bedroom were Teofilo and Ida. They felt exhausted. Teofilo was sulking and grumbling. He looked at his wife and said, "We are getting old, Ida. These were supposed to be our quiet years. I am seventy-eight; I always looked forward to my eightieth birthday. Do you think I'll make it?"

"Of course you will," said Ida.

"I always thought so, too. I have seen many things in my life, many, many things, but none like what we have seen in the last few years.

"Last night I had a dream. I forgot about it. All of a sudden, while I was listening to Angelo this evening, it came back to my mind. Maybe I should tell it to you before I go to sleep. I am almost afraid the dream will come back if I don't tell you. I am also afraid I'll forget it if I don't tell it to you right away."

"What did you dream?"

"I was a young accountant again. I don't know in which firm

I was working, but I was preparing the budget of the firm. It was very complicated. I felt I did not know how to do it. I was adding and adding, subtracting, dividing, and multiplying, and the result was always zero. I went to the boss and said, 'How is this possible? I have added and subtracted, divided and multiplied all these figures, and the result is always zero.' 'Don't you know algebra!' the boss said, angrily, furiously. 'You add and subtract what you did, and the result is zero, zero, zero, a gigantic zero.' I was seeing zeros all over, all around me. I woke up in a panic. I looked at you. I wanted to wake you up, but I fell asleep again. Today I forgot all about it until Angelo Luzzatto came in. Did he have to come here to disturb the peace of people older and wiser than he is? If he is right, we are in mortal danger. No matter how much we added and subtracted in our lives, we shall soon end in zero."

Ida said, "Don't be a fool, Teofilo. The zeros you saw are the beautiful zeros of Leonardo Fibonacci, the zeros that make thousands, millions, billions, and trillions. Don't let that impulsive young man disturb people like us, who have seen so many things in life. I tell you, nothing will happen to us. The proof of this is that nothing has happened until now. Don't you know who is here, in another room, close to us? The parnas. Where he is, nothing ending in zero could happen. Whatever will happen will be important. Listen to me, my dear husband. Pardo is not like the rest of us. He prays for us; he protects us. Teofilo, two more years to go and your age will have an eight and, next to it, a beautiful zero."

Teofilo looked at his wife with a smile that was also a "thank you." He kissed her, knowing that both of them would soon be able to sleep peacefully.

Next to theirs was the bedroom of Cesare, their son. He wanted to be near them, even at the age of forty-nine. He, too, was trying to make out the events of the day before he went to bed. That night he was very thoughtful, and yet he knew he could not think very much. People had told him time and time again that when he was a child he had had meningitis and that his brain had been injured. It was true. He remembered that as a young child he had been like the other children, but not after his illness. After his illness his schoolmates left him alone and did not seem to care for him anymore; now the whole world did not want to have anything to do with him, except for the people in Pardo's house.

He could not understand what was happening. Was it because of his illness that he could not understand what it was all about? But the others, too, did not seem to understand. Everything was so confused; everything seemed so crazy! What was that war people were always talking about? Why were buildings destroyed, people wounded, deported, killed? What was this being Jewish, this being Aryan, this being Fascist, this being Nazi, this being English, this being American? What was it all about? Maybe if he had not been ill, he could understand. And yet it seemed so easy to a person like him that these things should not happen. He wanted to be close to his parents, but many times he did not understand them either. Oh, how much better it would be if his sister Lucia were here! Now and then he listened to his Uncle Dario. Why wouldn't they let him work as a doctor any more? What had being Jewish to do with being a doctor? Why was Pisa cut in two right now? On one side of the Arno were the Americans; on the other side, the Germans. All the beautiful bridges had been destroyed. Nobody could cross the river. Would they build bridges again after the war? He hoped so much that they would. His home was on the other side of the Arno. Oh, how much he wished they would build the bridges again! He wanted to go home. The bridges! The bridges! He was glad Signor Pardo was here, on the same side of the river.

Next to Cesare's room was that of his Uncle Dario. And Dario, too, had to think again and again that night. The past seemed so long, so placid, so uneventful in comparison to this turbulent calm night. And now, out of that beautiful, almost amorphously beautiful, past certain episodes were emerging, like scary diabolical forms. One was the day he left the hospital. He had been called to city hall and bluntly told about the choice he had to make. "Either you belong to the Fascist party or you relinquish your hospital position."

"But what has belonging to a party to do with medicine?" he asked. No understanding from the mayor, the prefect, the commissioner of health when he went to talk to them. Each told him the same thing: "The choice is up to you." At that time Mussolini wanted every important person to join the party. Every intellectual was urged to become a member; it did not matter then whether the person was Christian or Jewish. There were even Jews who told Dario confidentially, "Our position is delicate. We who are such a tiny minority in Italy must show solidarity with the government, even a Fascist government." He was not persuaded. He found it necessary to stick to his principles . . . or what would be left? He was ousted from the hospital then. He did not have to wait like the other Jews who had joined the party and who had been kicked out of their positions when the government became openly anti-Semitic. He knew he had made the right decision, but what a price he had had to pay! He loved that hospital. He loved the building, the furniture, the beds, the nuns who ran the wards, the smell of medicine, the offices. Everything there had been carefully conceived and organized by him, and now he was being forced to leave.

Dario went on thinking, and a more recent day emerged in diabolic form from among his many recollections. It was the infamous July 15, 1938, when he had bought a newspaper at a newsstand and there, printed in large letters, he had read the *Manifesto della Razza,* a statement made under the aegis of the government by reputedly prominent scientists, which stated that Jews did not belong to the Italian race and had to be discriminated against. He remembered by heart the rhetorical emptiness of that manifesto, especially paragraph 9, the worst: "Of the Semites who, in the course of centuries have landed on the shores of our sacred fatherland, nothing has remained. Even the Arabic occupation of Sicily has left only a few names. The process of assimilation has been very rapid in Italy. The Jews represent the only population which has not been assimilated in Italy because the Jews consist of racial elements which are not European and are completely different from the elements which gave origin to the Italians."

He had understood immediately. This was the beginning of the end for the Jews of Italy. The so-called manifesto was a pseudoscientific statement designed to justify the Fascist government in following the Nazis by adopting the Nuremberg laws. Nor was he surprised; he had never harbored any illusions about the Fascist party. But who were the foolish clowns, masked as scientists, who would sign that ludicrous declaration? Who, in the name of science, would promote in Italy a huge wave of persecution? He looked at the names of those who had signed: Lino Businco, Lidio Cipriani, Leone Franzi, Guido Landra. They were obscure names that meant nothing. He continued to read and had one of the greatest shocks of his life: Nicola Pende had signed. Nicola Pende, the well-known physician, the famous endocrinologist whom Dario admired so much, whose lectures he had gone to Genoa to hear, whose writings he had avidly read and studied. How could a Pende sign such a shameful statement? Could it be that Mussolini had added Pende's name without consulting Pende? Improbable. Pende must have agreed, however reluctantly. Either he was afraid, or else he had yielded to the demonic appeal of power. But Dario Gallichi had not yielded.

Dario thought about what he had said to the guests at supper that evening, that the place where he most wanted to go after the war was the hospital. He had said that everything would take up again as it was before, as if nothing had happened. He let that fantasy fill his mind's eye. People would smile at him and say nothing on that beautiful day. They would act as if nothing had happened, and the nurse who always worked with him would go to the closet to get his white gown, with his name on it, and she would hand it to him . . . as if nothing had happened.

But he had another fantasy that the doctors, nurses, attendants, and patients would go to meet him and applaud and applaud. The rigid silence of many years would be broken at last. The nuns would even permit music to be played that day. Mother Superior would break all the rules and even dance with him. Would that be possible?

Which of the two fantasies was the better? He thought the first one was more eloquent in the imagined silence, but the second one was more fun! As if he were waking from a dream, he suddenly knew that neither one would come true. How terrible reality was without fantasy. Would he ever be in the hospital again? That was the place where he wanted to live, and when death came, that was the place where he wanted to die. He uttered a prayer to God: "Let me be in that hospital again; let me be in that hospital when I die."

Next door to Dario was the bedroom of the Levis. Ernesto entered and looked at Cesira. She was asleep. He tried to make no noise in order not to wake her. How beautiful she was in her sleep, more beautiful now than when she was a young woman. And how peacefully she could sleep! What a marvelous woman she was. True, she had a moment of weakness in Genoa that day when she wanted to give herself up, but since she had been in Pisa, she had been a source of strength. More than the other guests, she had understood what it meant to be in the house of the parnas. She had understood it more and more every day. He was slower than Cesira in grasping that meaning. That evening's discussion with Pardo had been an enlightenment. Would he be able to speak to Cesira about it? Probably not, but Cesira did not need to have things spelled out. She had a way of absorbing things as if by osmosis. Of course, if Cesira understood, it was because of what Pardo himself evoked. Oh, how much he had learned from Pardo, even that very evening. Yes, Pardo's two tragedies were both "nontragic" tragedies. At this point Ernesto thought of Angelo Luzzatto. If Angelo's life, too, ended in tragedy, it would also be a "nontragic" tragedy. Why, then, had Angelo been resented by the guests? After all, he was ready to fight evil with noble action. At least he tried to escape. But he was not touched by the Shekhinah. Pardo was.

Then images of Silvia came to Ernesto's mind—of her attentiveness, her loyalty, along with that of her helpers, Giovanna and Alice. Those three women must have been able to see Pardo's goodness; they must have found it to be as big as his helplessness. And they were remedying that helplessness with their own goodness.

Silvia, Giovanna, and Alice were also ready for bed. They had their own rooms on another floor, but since the six guests had come to live with Pardo, they had slept in the same room. Giovanna had not spoken too much the whole day. She looked at Silvia and said, "We're all tired. It's been a tiring day. Ever since Gilda came this morning with the message from her mother, you haven't been the same."

"I'm the same," said Silvia, "only a little more weary. I wish they'd leave us in peace, those neighbors of ours. They don't understand. I would never leave Signor Pardo. I told Gilda that. We're going to be liberated tomorrow. I'd never worry if these people didn't keep reminding us of all these troubles."

"Silvia," said Giovanna, "I'd never leave Signor Pardo either. Do you know how many years my husband and I worked in this house? I've lost count. Pasquino, God bless his soul, took the job as chauffeur when the horse and carriage were replaced by a car. Pasquino took Signor Pardo wherever he wanted to go, and Signor Pardo always went where Pasquino took him. When Pasquino passed away—God bless his soul—Signor Pardo told me, 'Giovanna, you lived here for many years when Pasquino was alive. You will continue to live here.' He did not put me out on the street. Should I leave him now, because of this trouble?"

"God forbid," said Silvia.

"But even after he told me I could stay, I said, 'Signor Pardo, I am so glad that you asked me to stay. But I'm no longer good at helping Silvia, and I will feel alone in this huge house. I have a sister, Alice. She, too, is alone.' And instantly Signor Pardo answered, 'Tell her to come to live here, too. There is room for her, also, in this house. She can lend Silvia a hand.'"

Alice then said, "Was I glad to be in this house, close to my sister. Signor Pardo is the one who opened a door for me. How could I leave him?"

"But you," said Giovanna turning to Silvia, "you have been here many years, I know. But still not so many as Pasquino and I. Yet you also want to stay."

"I do. You know who was here before me? Camilla. Camilla stayed with this family for over forty years, until she died of old age. All this political trouble does not change how people feel inside."

"Signor Pardo seems to need you, sometimes the way a little boy needs his mother."

"Sometimes he does seem helpless to me, and I feel inside I must help him. I'll help him as long as he lives, and as long as I live. Don't ask me why. I can only tell you it's so. But some of our neighbors have a hard time understanding."

"They don't understand," echoed Giovanna.

"They don't understand," repeated Alice.

Giovanna put out the candle and opened the window. The three women looked at the beautiful starry night, and the night seemed to understand.

Pardo in the Night of July 31

The house was now silent. Pardo felt it was time for him, too, to go to bed. Now the motions of his neurosis would begin to obtrude into the motionless calm of the night. Now the agony would repeat itself, because it was especially when he was about to go to bed that his fears would assail him with unrelenting ferocity. He had to go through the same routine every night. He had to check to make sure that no animals were in the closet, in the armoire, under the bed, behind other pieces of furniture; he had to listen carefully to convince himself that any indistinct noise was not the barking of a rabid dog or the howling of a wolf. So he entered the room resigned, waiting for his torturers to appear again, one by one.

But something most strange was happening. As he entered his bedroom, Pardo realized that he was not afraid. At first he did not give much importance to the fact: The fears might simply be late in appearing. He waited for them almost patiently, but they did not come. They seemed unwilling to reveal themselves. Almost to force their arrival, he looked at the closet and at the armoire, but he felt no need to open them. He looked at the bed but felt no need to look at the space between the mattress and the floor. He could not hear any suspicious noises. The night had entered its most silent hour. Yes, the night was calm, motionless, and of unusual beauty. He could not believe what was happening. He paced the room several times. Nothing! No fear! No fear! No fear! For the first time in his entire adult life at that time of night there was no fear, no terror. He wanted to give in to his joy by screaming. The impossible had occurred. "Why this?" he asked himself, and he found a prompt answer. The conversation with Ernesto, and perhaps with Angelo, too, had been a catharsis, had removed the purpose of the fears. He felt, however, that although that was a plausible idea, it was too simple an explanation. Free! Free! Free! The strange burden was shed, the obscure oppressor deposed. Could that be true? Again he felt like bursting into screams and shouting like a child who is overwhelmed by uncontrollable happiness, but he checked his impulse, not wanting to arouse the neighbors' attention. Free! Free! Free! No trembling, no hesitation. The enemy had faded away.

And now what? Why not call Ernesto again? He probably would not be asleep yet. Why not wake up everybody in the house? Tell them they could leave, vanish in various directions? There was no need to stay here, a place no longer assailed by neurotic danger but liable to be visited by catastrophe at any moment. We must all get out of here, he thought. It does not matter where. Now he could leave, now he had a choice. Now it was entirely up to him to stay or go. Now, he said to himself, using an expression familiar to him, for the first time he *coincided* with himself; that is, his psyche was no longer decreased or deprived of faculties. Whatever he decided to do, he would be totally accountable for it, as a person, as a parnas, as a believer in God. He had never felt so lucid, so capable of thinking fast in various directions, and he had to think fast, because soon he had to make the final decision. The idea occurred to him that the absence of fear might be only an interlude, a deceptive one. The fears might return, as intense as before, or more so. And yet he had an intuitive presentiment that the fears would never return. What about the maids? They could be forced to go to a neighbor's home. What about his Jewish guests? Were he to wake them up, he would scare them and break the belief to which they clung so tenaciously and dearly. But was their mysticism completely unfounded, or was it based on something that at the time nobody could understand?

Could it be that he was no longer possessed by fantastic fears because he sensed that real danger was approaching? He remembered reading that neurotic and psychotic people at times lose their imaginary obsessions and fears in situations that are realistically dangerous. He stopped thinking for a while. He tried to thin out the ideas that were crowding his head. Then he proceeded again in his thinking by slow and calm steps.

He had reached the point at which the mysteries of life required a metaphysical, not a psychological explanation. He did not have the feeling that destiny was closing in. His destiny was being realized, was finding actualization. He must face his destiny and discover the meaning of his life. Without that discovery his life was neither important nor significant in a way he wanted it to be. If for almost six decades he had been kept in a state of oppression by his fears, that state must be a significant one. And now he must continue to pursue the pattern of his life by choice, in search of that still-hidden significance. Perhaps that was what God wanted. Now God gave him the privilege of choosing. He thought again about Ernesto's remark that "The Shekhinah may require illness"; it occurred to him that Silvia and her two helpers, and the six guests, had already chosen to stay. Now it was his time to choose; now he chose to stay.

He opened the window facing the garden and looked up at the vault of the heavens. It was the night of July 31, full of stars, a night when shooting stars add to the triumph of the sky. So many! And in so many directions, leaving burning wakes that festooned corners of the darkness with festive fires. Shooting stars calling for wishes to be made! Of course, the wish that Fascism would fall. The firmament was proclaiming the end of the tyranny.

The stars were silently singing a celestial hymn, which was heard by the whole universe, a hymn that linked the majesty of God to the forthcoming emancipation. The heavens were receiving now no anxious sighs, but hopeful wishes of freedom. The eternal beauty was there, reaffirming the eternal truth, the great Shekhinah, the Divine Presence.

Would the Divine Presence permit the revelation of his personal mystery? And in what way? But one thing he had firmly established. He was not a helpless spectator of cosmic events. He had decided; he had chosen. The greatness of his ability to choose seemed to him attuned to the greatness of the universe. In the acknowledgment of this ability, his joy at being a man was not a sign of presumptuousness.

Pardo saw that the brevity of our days is blessed by a fleeting glimpse of things that are eternal, and the burden of the spirit is blessed by the anticipation of liberation—any liberation being an advancement of the human soul to be transmitted to future generations. This type of advancement had been happening for a long time, since the days of the slavery in Egypt.

The nostalgia for infinity, which is never quenched in the human being, was at this point somehow changed to serene contemplation and meditation. Thoughts came to Pardo in the form of metaphors. He reflected that if the earth were always in daylight, people would not know the night and the infinity of the universe. Astronomy would not have evolved. Thus darkness can bring about enlightenment. And the darkness of evil can bring about the shining of goodness. Darkness and evil may be necessary but not enough, just as the sun and the moon and the stars are not enough for enlightenment. To overcome the horizon of darkness the Divine Presence is necessary. And Pardo thought again of Isaiah:

The sun shall be no more
your light by day,
nor for brightness shall the moon

give light to you;
but the Lord will be your everlasting light
and your God will be your glory.[1]

How would the earth appear to people living in other parts of the firmament? Could what Angelo said be true, that astronomers from other solar systems would call the earth the Infamous Planet, perhaps the Planet of Adolf Hitler? No, thought Pardo, in the most resolute way. Why not the planet of Homer, Dante, and Shakespeare? Of Moses, Buddha, and Jesus? For him, Giuseppe Pardo Roques, this was the planet of Abraham, the son of Terah, of the land of Ur, Abraham, who was told by God on a starry night to look toward heaven and count the stars. But he could not. So many were the works of God, and so many would be the descendants of Abraham, the descendants who would learn from Abraham to distinguish the majesty of the creation from the greater majesty of the Creator. This was Abraham's planet for Giuseppe Pardo Roques.

The parnas then diverted his attention from the sky to himself, and started to review his whole life: the time when he was vicemayor of Pisa, and when he was the chief administrator of the congregation of Pisa, including the synagogue and the parochial school, and his dealings with the students of the university who had come from foreign countries, and his embracing of the Zionist cause in order to help persecuted Jews go to the land of Israel. He could also add that he had tried to follow Isaiah[2] and had shared his bread with the hungry and brought the homeless to his house, irrespective of whether the hungry and the homeless were Christians or Jews. He reviewed the errors, misunderstandings, wrong decisions that he had made; and he concluded that he could accept all of them now. There was peace in his spirit,

1. Isaiah 60:19.
2. Isaiah 58:7.

and with that peace was a calm joy. However, an additional decision had to be made—whether to wake up the guests—not to tell them to leave, but to inform them about what had happened to him. He concluded that he should not. He felt that whatever had gone on inside him that night was meant for him, was clear only to him, and was probably impossible to communicate at that particular time. He could not present to the guests any definite, clear-cut conclusion, any idea that had even a remote connection with tangible reality. He should go to bed and sleep. In a few moments he would fall asleep in the most calm, restful way. His sleep would contain no dreams. No dreams were needed to carry the burden of grieved desires or of no-longer-threatening threats. The great desire was about to be fulfilled. Fascism was about to end.

All of a sudden, a sound. The pulse of life intruded again into the night. Yes, it was distinctly recognizable, although distant, as the barking of a dog. He knew that barking, which was coming from the house of a not-too-close neighbor, the barking that had made him tremble so many times. But not that night. That night the barking was the barking of a dog. He listened keenly. The barking was not menacing but moaning, wailing, almost as if it lamented something that had happened or was about to happen. Giuseppe felt sorry for the dog. And by association of ideas he thought of the poem by Umberto Saba about a goat, alone in the meadow, tied and rain-sodden. The goat was bleating, and the monotonous bleat sounded to the poet like his own grief. The poet spoke to the goat in mockery first, but then in earnest "because sorrow is eternal and has only one and unvarying voice." In the bleating of that goat, who had a "Semitic muzzle," the poet, a Jew, heard "the lamenting of all living creatures." Sorrow includes animals and humans in one big fraternity. Let us not divide the creatures of God into smaller categories. Pardo thought that that dog, barking in the distance, was the friend of man.

At this point he bent his head down toward the garden and saw many tiny lights, here and there, reminiscent of the bigger lights in the sky. They were the fireflies that occasionally visited his garden. Neither the stars nor the fireflies were respecting the curfew of darkness that night. The garden was still flourishing, he thought, in spite of the summer drought. He could not see the colors of the flowers, but the various fragrances reached him. And again Isaiah entered his mind:

> And you shall be like a watered garden,
> like a spring of water, whose waters fail not.[3]

Perhaps, he thought, that was why he wanted that garden to be well tended, because a garden was a symbol of the way he tried to be, in accordance with the words of the prophet.

At this point a strident thought suddenly began to nag at him. Enrico Giordano! A neighbor and a tenant of his, living in the house next door to the abandoned one. Although Giordano lived one flight up, he had wanted to use the garden, which was usually given to the family living on the first floor, in this case the Palagini family. Giordano often spoke to Pardo on the street in a friendly way, but that garden had remained to this day an object of contention. Why would such an irrelevant and inconsequential thought occur to him just then? Why did the name "Enrico Giordano" keep recurring in his mind? Pardo concluded that it was because he was thinking about the garden, and how everybody, including the Palagini and the Giordano families, appreciated the joy of a garden.

Not only did the fresh aroma reach him, but also the sound of the fountain. It flowed all the time, like a brook, like a spring that fails not. It was there, also, to indicate that the well was full and could provide water for his home and for the homes of the neighbors. Tomorrow morning the good neighbors would come again for their daily supply.

3. Isaiah 58:11.

Angelo in the Pinewood

When Angelo left Pardo's house, he looked up and down Sant'
Andrea Street: no sign of life in the short street, both ends of
which he could see. He walked firmly along the sidewalk, close
to the buildings, turned rapidly three or four times onto streets
still familiar from the days of his youth, and in less than fifteen
minutes was in Santa Caterina Square. At a corner of the square
was the ancient church, and there, almost indistinguishable in
the darkness, a man. Angelo looked at him attentively, but with
an assumed indifference.

The stranger said, "What do you have to say?"

Angelo whispered, "Carlo and Nello." Those were the passwords.

"Carlo and Nello," whispered the man in the darkness, eager
to reassure. And the words, because of their heartening effect and
because of what they signified—the first names of the Rosselli
brothers, murdered by the Fascists—seemed as vast as Pisa's noc-
turnal silence and as bright as rays of light piercing a besieging
blackness.

Angelo looked at the man closely and was struck by his youth
and simple appearance. He was in his early twenties and was
dressed like a person coming from the country. "Follow me," he
said. Angelo followed trustingly, and the two walked through the

narrow streets to a point where, crossing the walls of the city, they were to proceed to an overgrown field where two bicycles had been hidden. Everything went according to plan. In twenty minutes they reached the field, and there were the two bicycles, untouched, covered by bushes.

"Pay attention," said the young man. "We must avoid the regular roads and take short-cuts and paths between fields, where we are not likely to meet anybody. Some of the paths are only footpaths, so be careful not to fall. I don't think we'll meet anybody; but if somebody does try to stop us, I'm ready," and he pointed to a sheathed dagger on his right side. The dagger convinced Angelo at last that the war had finally started for him, too. He was there, in earnest, ready.

They got on the bicycles, the young man a few feet ahead. The paths were irregular and bumpy, with stones and grass making them barely discernible. Angelo felt several times at first that he was about to fall, but he soon noted with satisfaction that he was managing very well on the practically nonexistent paths. His eyes grew adjusted to the darkness, and he began to distinguish various objects. The sky was filled with stars, and they helped, too.

Soon the country fields, uncultivated because of the war, gave way to the pinewood of San Rossore, a forest once reserved for the exclusive use of the royal family. The young man and Angelo were now able to travel on regular paths, easily recognizable even if they were the smallest in the wood and known only to a few. The two men could ride at great speed. Riding, in fact, became so easy that Angelo found himself carried away by his thoughts.

Bice came into his mind, and he remembered that he had not always been true to her. He had never revealed his infidelity to anyone. He had been about to speak to Pardo of it earlier that evening, but he had decided not to do so. The whole affair had seemed trivial to him, especially in the midst of the world events. He had been in Nice on a business trip and had met this Frenchwoman. He was taken by her frivolous, merry ways. He was supposed to be in Nice only a week, but he had stayed longer and had returned to Nice several times after that on one pretext or another. Bice was a serious woman. He loved her dearly, but Denise had succeeded in adding spice and fun to life. All this had been before the war. It seemed centuries ago. He had not been in touch with Denise for several years, and he had no desire to resume contact with her. In fact, he had almost forgotten the affair, except when the little adventure reappeared to him as a faint memory.

He had felt no guilt about it, he thought, brought up as he was in a society where the double standard prevailed. But now that Bice had been taken away, he did feel guilty. His deceit, which he had conveniently dismissed as minor, appeared to him as far more blameworthy now, when he thought about Bice's fate. And that was not right either. He should not ennoble his petty guilt by associating it with Bice's destiny. The best thing to do was to forget completely what had happened in Nice and to concentrate on Bice, on how beautiful their love had been, in spite of his infraction. He should remember their honeymoon in Sicily, and the birth of Liana, and the happy years they had had together in Parma.

Bice, Bice, Bice. She kept reappearing in his mind, with her smile, her tender ways, her kisses, her determined resolutions, her keen mind, her various interests, her slim figure, her quivering breasts, her bright eyes, her vivacious movements, and yet with the pensive mood into which she frequently fell whenever she was trying to guess what could possibly happen. Angelo was bicycling fast, trying to keep up with the young man, while his thoughts kept going back, far in the past, to the old dreams, to Bice's smile, and to Liana.

A leaf fell from a tree. "Bice, are you calling me?" Angelo thought.

In the surrounding darkness invisible but friendly eyes seemed to turn toward him. "Bice, are you looking at me?"

Invisible hands seemed to touch his shoulder while he was bicycling. "Bice, are you touching me?"

Then Bice, too, faded from his mind. As the bicycles took them farther and farther away from Pisa, his thoughts went back to Pardo's words, especially those he had not fully understood. What had Pardo meant when he said that fate becomes an inward necessity? Perhaps he knew now. Was his fate, like the fate of many Jews, directing him to this dangerous adventure, or was it rather an inner mandate that he could not disregard if he wanted to feel true to himself?

On each side of the path now the pines became taller and taller, no longer like shadows, but like bodyguards that silently accompanied him all the way. They seemed to lift his thoughts and him, too, in their vertical aiming at the sky.

Angelo tried to evoke again the mystical spirit of Pardo. Maybe the parnas meant that one's fate and course of life must spring from faith, not from despair. Angelo could recognize in himself now an inward necessity, the invisible guiding force that with an uncanny clarity makes us choose one path and avoid another, irrespective of what the result will be. But how was it possible to have faith in those tragic moments and to follow Pardo's suggestion "to let hope grow in our hearts, like roses in a garden, and not leave room only for the weed of despair?" The weed of despair was everywhere. Hitler and his army of Cains had sown it all over.

Angelo looked around, and again the night seemed black all over, infinitely. Doubts made him tremble, like a young tree shaken by the wind. But the pines on both sides of the path were unfaltering in their vertical stance.

By now they had reached a river. The young man said, "This is the Serchio River. We'll cross, then enter the pinewood of Migliarino. From now on we must walk. It's not far. We'll hide the bicycles here. I need one to go back."

Using a boat that had been hidden in the foliage drooping from the bank, they crossed the river. They walked for about a mile, Angelo carrying his sack. Then the young man stopped and said, "We're too early. We must arrive at the sailboat at exactly 2:00 A.M. Let's stop here for a while and rest."

The two of them stopped and sat on the ground. Angelo said, "You're so young. Why are you willing to risk your life to help me cross the line?"

"I'm not so young; I'm twenty-three, and I've already been called into the Army four times by those Fascists in the North. But I'll never fight on the side of the Nazis. So you see, I'm a fugitive, too. I'm a partisan."

"Do you know anything about me?"

"I don't even know your name. I'm not supposed to ask your name, and you're not supposed to ask mine. I know only that you are a Jew."

"How did you happen to be assigned to me?"

"They were distributing missions at our command post. When I heard that one was helping a Jew to cross the line, I volunteered."

"Why?"

"I had never seen a Jew before. No, I should be more precise. A Jew was the first person I ever saw in my life, and from then until now I have not seen another one but you. I know you don't understand what I am saying. You see, I come from the village of Vecchiano. Only one Jewish family has ever lived there since the world was created. It was the family of a doctor named Elio Arieti. When my mother was about to give birth to me, she had a lot of trouble, and the midwife had already given me up for lost. They called Dr. Arieti. He came, and he worked hard the whole night, and here I am. My mother and father always spoke to me about this doctor, this Jew, and so did our friends Nella, Furimma, and Gigia." He paused for a while, and then, as if struck by a sudden thought, he said, "The doctor had two sons. I remember the name of the older one: Silvano. The doctor and his family moved to Pisa. Say, are *you* Silvano Arieti?"

"No, no," said Angelo. "I cannot tell you who I am, but I am not Silvano Arieti. Silvano is at least five years younger than I. He is a doctor, too, like his father. He specializes in mental diseases. I don't know where his parents are, but he went to America. I suppose he has a much easier time than we do; he is an olive that will remain on the olive tree."

"An olive? That's funny. How can a person be an olive?"

"Please excuse me; I was reminding myself of a conversation I just had with a learned man. He said that in the Bible it is written that when the winds of a storm blow through an olive grove, most of the olives fall and are wasted, but it is not so bad after all. A few remain on the trees, just as some men remain alive after a war. And with the olives that remain, we can plant new olive groves."

"What you say makes no sense to me. People who have gone to school for a long time say one thing and mean another. But olives are something I know very well. Vecchiano is surrounded by hills, all covered by olive groves. We are proud of them. And no storm has ever been so strong as to make most of Vecchiano's olives fall. God forbid! We farmers and workers in the field, we don't think about olive groves for the future. For us, an olive lost counts. We don't want to lose even one."

The words of the young peasant caught Angelo's imagination. Now he understood how the young man, and Silvia, and probably most Christians, could not live according to the passage in Isaiah. Perhaps only a Jew could understand. The Christian way of living is the normal and natural one. An olive lost counts as a loss, and the pain of the poor adolescent Annina counts as a pain. Fortunate indeed were the people of Vecchiano and all those who, unlike the children of Israel, are not hit by such huge storms, and don't heed only cataclysms, and don't think that a raft with a few shipwrecked persons counts more than the lost ship.

But then why should a Jew let hope grow like roses in a garden? How can he have room for anything but the weed of despair? Angelo felt he finally understood what Pardo had meant. The hope must be placed in the olives that are saved; our despair can become faith if we think, live, and act chiefly for them. Thus hope becomes a translucent essence: the perennial creation of life through rebirth, and the resilient resourcefulness of the human being. Hope is an attitude in which the future is more intensely present than the present, and in which what is good for the group and the group's ideals lies above one's desires.

"Can I talk to you? We have a few more minutes before we go," said the young man. He had realized that Angelo needed to be alone with his thoughts for a while.

"Please talk," replied Angelo.

"I want to tell you something about this pinewood. It belongs to the duke—I mean the Duke Salviati. Normally I divide my work between the farm in Vecchiano, not far from here, and my work in the wood, for the duke. But since I am a draft evader, I spend a lot of time in the wood, which I have known since I was a boy. There is no tree here that I don't know, no bush that I don't recognize. Most of the trees are pines. They all seem alike; they all grow and become quite high. But in fact they do not grow in the same way. Each one tells the story of the time since it was planted.

"Look at that one, how tall it is. It wants to be taller than the others and reach the fresh air above, and the first sun in the morning. Do you realize how high and slim and straight it is? Over twelve meters. The other one, not so high, prefers to be fatter in its trunk. This other one bends; it does not know whether to grow east toward the mountains or west toward the sea, and the other one is so contorted, as if it went through many troubles to find its space in the wood. And look at that little one over there, shy and small. Far at the right you see a group of them, in a row. They look alike, like soldiers ready to march. But they will stay there forever. I tell you for sure I know each pine of the wood. I could give a name to each of them. They have tried to plant different trees around here, especially near the beach—palms, eucalyptus, mimosa, aloes, junipers, mastic trees. But they can never take over.

This is the land of the pine. The sea spray is to the pine what the dew is to other plants."

As the young man spoke, the wood became populated for Angelo not by shadows, but by living trees. And in spite of the stillness of the night and the almost imperceptible wind, he could hear a gentle rustling.

The young man continued. "This pinewood goes as far as Viareggio, where it joins the linden trees. There are all kinds of animals, even deer, and all kinds of birds. I know all of them. And do you hear those sounds, like steps of people? They are not people; they are boars. Our boars are black like coal. They stay together in families; we can recognize the father, the mother, and the little ones."

Angelo was intent, looking back and forth between the young man's almost illuminated face and the woods he knew so intimately, looking for all that life his companion was celebrating, as it were, with his very being. He tried to hear the birds and animals through the stillness.

"Not these days, of course," continued the young man, "but before the war, young men and women used to come here at night during the summer to sing and dance. Girls came from all over, not only Vecchiano, but Nodica, San Giuliano, Migliarino, Torredel-Lago, Ponte-a-Serchio—though believe me, the best looking ones came from Vecchiano. What a time we used to have!"

Angelo paid close attention, and every word he heard was full of color and sound. For him, too, the wood became inhabited by nymphs and satyrs. Bice no longer existed, nor did any trace of that so-fresh sorrow. How superficial he had been, Angelo thought, to have found such a young man's way of living superficial. What the young man was really doing was creating an eternal present that he might give to himself and others—and he was doing so in spite of the war.

But the war, banished from their spirits for a few minutes, returned. "It is fifteen minutes to two," said the young man. "We must go." The two resumed their march. They moved toward the beach, and a great long strip of sand appeared, off-white even in the dark of night. Soon something resembling a human figure began to appear standing next to something shaped like a boat.

Angelo could not resist the impulse to look back at the woods, still full of the promise of nymphs and satyrs, laughter and songs, birds and boars. He felt a powerful urge to go back, to forget everything and stay hidden among the pines for the duration of the war. For the first time he understood the meaning of the Italian word *imboscato,* a man who evades army service by going into a *bosco,* a wood. The *imboscato* not only avoids the ugliness of war, on the one side, but he can positively enjoy the beauty of the wood on the other. The pines seemed to be whispering to Angelo, "Come back! Be one of us. Forget the future. Come back to the eternal present." But the inward necessity made itself felt again, and fate resumed its forward course. Angelo and the young man hurried toward the person near the boat.

The stranger was a man in his forties with an almost impassive face. "What do you want?" he snapped as the two men approached.

"Carlo and Nello," said Angelo.

"Carlo and Nello," echoed the young man from Vecchiano.

"Carlo and Nello," replied the stranger, and his face changed in the direction of a faint smile.

"Are you set to go?" he asked Angelo.

"I am," Angelo replied.

The man explained how to use the sailboat.

"Why is the sail such a dark gray?" asked Angelo.

"So as not to be seen in the night," answered the stranger. "But by dawn you will have crossed the line, and you'll want to be seen by the Allies. Then you must change the sail. If the Fascist marine police catch you, do you know what to say?"

"Yes, that I am a fisherman."

"You will show them the net that we put in the boat. We also put in some fish, which you will say is your catch. Have you any identification papers?"

"None whatsoever."

"That's good. But you know, it can happen that we think we have no identification and yet we have forgotten something that can identify us."

"Before reaching Pisa I changed all my clothes; there is absolutely nothing in the sack that can identify me."

"You're sure you can sail?"

"In my youth I used to spend summers in Viareggio, and I am quite competent with a boat."

"Good," said the stranger. "Then everything is ready. Get into the boat; we'll push you off the shore."

"Good luck," said the young man, shaking hands with Angelo.

"The wind be with you," said the stranger.

Angelo thanked them and jumped onto the boat.

The wind was dying down. The boat moved slowly, as if pushed only by the passenger's heartbeat, or by his inward necessity and fate.

Dawn of August 1

As usual, Cesare was the first one awake, shortly after dawn, when the birds began to chirp. He had never learned to distinguish which bird was which. Swallows? Sparrows? Blackcaps? The birds liked the garden and assembled there, but nobody ever woke up or listened to them except Cesare. He had been waking up early since he was a child, especially after his illness, when he would wake up feeling a wild restlessness, needing to move around, to go into other rooms and wake up his family. But the others, the adults, always said, "Stay in your bedroom, Cesare. Don't make so much noise; we want to sleep." And he had learned to be quiet.

Those adults! Why did they want to sleep so late? Why did the birds waken only him? Did it have something to do with his illness? Probably. He had been surprised at how many things had been connected with his illness. Would he grow up? Would he ever be able to talk to the others, to talk the way they did? Every morning he had to stay alone in his room. The birds were there, and he listened to them. But to them, too, he had nothing to say. Were they saying something to him? Probably many things, but he didn't know how to put into words what they were saying. Lately, however, he knew for sure one thing they said: "We birds are not afraid." Everybody else was afraid of something—of the war, of people, of the Nazis, the Fascists, the planes, the bombs, the soldiers, the police. Why was everybody afraid? If he hadn't had meningitis, he would understand why. At any rate, he, too, had become afraid like the others.

He was not a complete idiot; he knew that the Nazis, the Fascists, the police, the soldiers, the planes, the bombs, the cannons, the rifles were there to hurt. And yet he had also heard that at times you don't have to be afraid, even though you are. He had heard that Pardo was afraid of what he should not be afraid of. Pardo himself had said so the night before. And he had heard people whispering that Pardo was mentally ill, just like him, Cesare, after the meningitis. Everybody looked up to Pardo, but down on Cesare. Why, if they were both ill? Everybody seemed willing to keep quiet about Pardo's illness, but not about Cesare's. To excuse him for not being able to do what other people did, his mother used to say, "My poor Cesare had meningitis when he was a little boy." Often she added, "But he understands. You'll be surprised at how many things he understands."

His mother loved him, he knew; his father loved him, he was sure; and uncle Dario, the doctor, cared so much for him. He was lucky to be with them. Oh, if only his sister Lucia were there with them, in Pardo's home! In Pardo's home there was nothing to be afraid of, because all fears were like Pardo's fears. Pardo was a very unusual man. They were lucky to be with him.

The sun was rising, and the birds were twittering less and less. That was a reminder. Soon it would be time to turn on the radio. The radio's voice was the opposite of the singing of the birds. It was the voice of fear. The radio always talked about things to be afraid of. Nevertheless, it had become Cesare's hobby to hear the first news of the morning, when everyone was sleeping, and then report it to the other people in the household. At 6:30 A.M., not every morning, but every two or three days, some electricity was made available by the authorities so that people could listen to the news and learn the orders given by the military command.

Cesare had learned to listen only to the local Fascist station because, according to a law promulgated during the war, anyone caught listening to an enemy station would be severely punished.

Cesare had found out that when he reported the news to the other members of the household, they paid careful attention to what he said and then most of the time concluded that what he had heard was a bunch of Nazi and Fascist lies, like the news that the Germans were winning everywhere in Russia, in Africa, and in the south of Italy, and that the war would soon be over. Oh, if only it were true! Then he, Cesare, could cross the Arno again and go back to his home. When would the war be over? Tomorrow, maybe?

6:30 A.M. Time for the news. He turned on the radio, and it lit up. Wonderful! Electricity was available that morning! That day he would have something to report. "Giornale Radio," the station announced. "Early morning news. Long live *Il Duce*." Then the Fascist anthem. Yes, the radio again announced that soon the Allies would be pushed out of the south of Italy. On the Eastern front the Russians had been defeated everywhere. The Japanese were conquering the entire Pacific Ocean. Gigantic losses had been inflicted on English and American forces. Would he be able to remember, Cesare thought. Would he be able to repeat all this news to his parents, his uncle, the Levis, and Signor Pardo?

Then the radio added, "Attention! Attention for the latest local news. This morning, a few hours before dawn, a man attempted to defect to the enemy by boat." A sense of foreboding crept through Cesare. His hearing sharpened; his heart raced; his body quivered. And he did not even know why. The radio continued, "The defector was suspected of being a Jew and was killed on the spot." Cesare was shaking now. Why did he feel that way? Because of Angelo? But he had no reason to think that Angelo wanted to cross the line. He had heard similar news almost every time the radio functioned. There was always somebody who had unsuccessfully tried to cross the line. But this time the radio had said that the trespasser was a Jew. Jews were often blamed for things they had not done. Could it be that this time, too, the news was a lie? After all, Cesare had been told many times that he did not know when a lie was a lie. For him, nobody ever lied.

Cesare looked at his watch. Not even 7:00. He would have to wait a long time before reporting what he had heard. Uncle Dario, who was usually the first to wake up, wouldn't get up before 7:30. Would Cesare be able to wait? He had to wait. He shouldn't wake up the others so early in the morning. He should remember that people who had not had meningitis do not wake up so early. The birds had completely stopped twittering, and the sun was already strong. Cesare thought that it would be a very hot day.

Early Morning of August 1

On the morning of August 1, everyone in Pardo's house got up early, as was customary during the hot days of Italian summer. Pardo seemed more cheerful, more lively, more hopeful than usual and tried to impart that feeling to his six guests, who, this time, did not respond to his mood. He thought they had no reason to feel better, since, unlike him, they had not had the fervid experience of the previous night, and therefore he accepted the way they were. He also had the feeling that for some inexplicable reason he was irritating them, so he decided to leave them alone in the room where they were having breakfast. As soon as he had left, Dario said, "Giuseppe seems happy this morning. We did the right thing in not telling him."

"What was there to tell?" asked Cesira, who also seemed to be unaware of what was troubling some of them.

"Tell them what you heard this morning on the radio," Dario said to Cesare. Cesare reported almost verbatim the radio's announcements. The Allies would soon be repulsed from the south of Italy. On the Eastern front the Russians were defeated everywhere. The Japanese were conquering the entire Pacific Ocean. Gigantic losses had been inflicted on English and American forces.

Nobody was paying careful attention to what Cesare was reciting, the same familiar version of the military situation that was broadcast month after month. "Cesare," Dario urged, "tell us what you heard about the local news."

Cesare stuttered a little. "They said a man had tried to cross the line and was killed. They said it may be a Jew."

"Was any name mentioned, any locality?" asked Ernesto.

"No," replied Cesare.

"That person may not be a Jew. They may have said that for propaganda," said Dario. "There is no reason for us to think that the person was Angelo. Nevertheless, it is unhappy news. Maybe the dead man *was* a Jew."

"You see," said Teofilo, "I am right. The least risk is in remaining here. This is not a completely safe place, but it is less risky than elsewhere. Were we to leave, we would immediately fall into the hands of the Germans, like ripe plums."

Ida wished to strengthen the position taken by her husband. "This place is not just less risky; it is a safe place. I wish my daughter were here. If they wanted to get us, they would have already done so. This house is marked by God for a special purpose." Her mystical view was by now openly pragmatic. Any reminder of the inhospitable, inimical, and cruel world reinforced her vision of Pardo's house as a holy spot. For her husband, Pardo's house was a relatively safe spot, as safe as a raft can be in the middle of a rough ocean, when the only alternative is to be amid the waves.

"Why don't you want Giuseppe to know what Cesare heard on the radio?" Cesira asked Dario.

"We do not know who the defector is," replied Dario, and in his doctor's capacity added, "There is no point in upsetting him. Anyhow, Giuseppe generally listens to the radio at ten o'-clock. Maybe the announcement will be repeated then in greater detail."

Hesitation overtook the guests. They had allowed themselves to be led by Dario, but they were not completely convinced. Of one thing they were very much afraid, without openly admitting it, and that was of changing Pardo's mood. If he became anxious or depressed or felt hopeless, the whole atmosphere in his home would change, and panic would spread among them. Again they had to hold on to that raft with all the strength they could muster.

Moreover, if Pardo were told the news, there would be nothing he could do; nor could he find out for sure whether the slain Jew was Angelo. Generally the radio did not report news about captured Jews. As a matter of fact, a wall of silence was kept about the destiny of those who were deported. In relation to Italian Jews the words "concentration camp" were never used. Instead, such places were called *campi di raccolta*, which means camps where people are gathered together, with no implication of bad treatment whatsoever. If the radio had given the news that a Jew had been killed, there was a special point to be made, that the Jew had wanted to do something inimical to the Nazi-Fascist cause; for instance, to join the Allied forces.

The guests dropped the whole topic. Nevertheless, they remained restless and fidgeted, far more so than the previous night when they had gone to bed. But not so with Pardo.

Pardo was more than serene. Nothing seemed to indicate to him the tightening of the circle. As if he were totally oblivious of the war, he went into his study to read. He used to alternate between contemporary books and biblical, talmudic, or classical studies. That morning he decided to reread a part of Ecclesiastes. He was still under the influence of the book of Isaiah, which last night had pervaded his mind; now it was also Ecclesiastes that was impinging on all his thoughts. How can these two books of the Bible, so different, be reconciled? Isaiah reaffirms the great values, universal brotherhood and the mark of the eternal; the author of Ecclesiastes tells us that everything is transient and comes and goes: "All things are full of weariness";[1] "There is noth-

---

1. Ecclesiastes 1:8.

ing new under the sun";[2] "Vanity of vanities! All is vanity."[3] How can such skepticism about life be connected with the deep attributes given to life by the prophets, the Pentateuch, or the Talmud? He remembered the statement of Renan[4] that Ecclesiastes in the midst of the Bible is like a small essay by Voltaire lost in a theological library. And yet he felt that Ecclesiastes portrayed very well the unceasing struggle of the living and that it suggested accepting the cyclical course of everything under the sun. "There is a time for war and a time for peace, a time to be born and a time to die." As in many previous times, he was particularly struck by the verse, "I praised the dead which are already dead more than the living which are yet alive."[5] The dead had already gone through the trial of living and had already accepted whatever life had brought to them. Pardo was wondering whether it was possible to see a link between the skepticism of this book and the holy certitude of the other books of the Bible when Silvia knocked at the door.

"Signor Pardo, don't worry if the bell rings soon or if you hear a knock at the door downstairs. From the window I saw Mrs. Del Francia and Mr. Ristori coming here for the water." She meant that two neighbors were already coming for a supply of water from the garden well. Others would soon follow.

"Very well," said Pardo, smiling. The daily occurrence had become almost a pleasant ritual, and that day it seemed even more pleasant. It confirmed once more that there were some people who did not heed the government's propaganda and were willing to maintain relations with Jews.

Pardo went downstairs to greet the neighbors. There was an exchange of cordiality—"Good morning, how are you?"—and

2. Ecclesiastes 1:9.
3. Ecclesiastes 1:2.
4. Renan, E., *Histoire du Peuple d'Israel* (Paris: Cahuann-Levy, 1923), vol. 5, chap. 5.
5. This passage from Ecclesiastes (4:2) is engraved on Pardo's tombstone in the Jewish cemetery of Pisa.

general comments about the fact that last night was very quiet, with no noise of cannons, planes, or troop movements. Silvia then directed the two neighbors to go into the garden, carrying their containers.

It was about ten o'clock, and Pardo remembered it was time for the news. Cesare turned on the radio. They were all gathered in the living room except for the neighbors, who were in the garden. The guests were particularly interested in knowing whether any additional news would be given about the man who was killed while trying to cross the line. The radio lit again that day. The first few items of news were about the war and conveyed the usual distorted information, with the intent of making the listeners believe that the Nazi-Fascist Axis would sooner or later attain victory. Finally a local item was given.

"More information about the man who tried to cross over to the Allies in a sailboat. Marine officers found him a few miles from the shore, between the mouths of the Serchio and the Arno Rivers, appproximately an hour before dawn. It would not have been possible to identify him except for the fortunate circumstance that one of the marine officers was a high school classmate of the captured man. The officer recognized him as a Jew named Angelo Luzzatto. The transgressor was killed on the spot. His body is now at the bottom of the sea, where it deserves to be." Then there was a signal, followed by the sentences with which the broadcast was usually ended:

Il Duce is always right.
Remember his words:
To believe, to obey, to fight.[6]

6. In the original Italian:
Il Duce ha sempre ragione.
Ricordate le sue parole:
Credere, obbedire, combattere.

Cesare turned off the radio. All the listeners were frozen, but soon it was clear that Pardo was more disturbed than the others. Whereas the others soon reacquired their composure, he did not. During the war people used to hear so much bad news that they had become almost accustomed to it. Why did Pardo continue to be so upset? Why would he not talk? The guests started to consider what would happen to them if Giuseppe remained that way. They gathered around him and tried to console him, at first with soft, affectionate whispering, then with louder compassionate words. Even the two neighbors came in from the garden when they heard the dismayed voices from inside the house. Silvia, Alice, and Giovanna also joined the group in the living room. Everyone wanted to help, but they did not know how. Ernesto managed to say, "This is one more trial, Giuseppe," but Pardo did not reply.

He couldn't talk. He was rapidly reviewing in his mind what he believed in most and was battling with emerging doubts while his heart was sobbing. And now Angelo, Angelo, too, was felled by the storm. Would any remain on the old tree? Could it be that none would? Could he understand now the prophet Habakkuk's challenge to God?

> How long, O Lord, shall I cry
> And Thou wilt not hear?
> I cry out unto Thee of violence
> And Thou wilt not save.[7]

No, no; he must believe in Jeremiah, who spoke of a covenant of love not to be engraved on stone but to be written in human hearts after the huge destruction. No, no; he must believe in Isaiah, who saw the day when

. . . the wolf shall dwell with the lamb,

7. Habakkuk 1:2.

And the leopard shall lie down with the kid;
And the calf and the young lion and the fatling together;
And a little child shall lead them.[8]

No, no; he must believe in Ezekiel, who reported the voice of God:

Yet will I leave a remnant, in that ye shall
have some that escape the sword among the
nations, when ye shall be scattered
through the countries.[9]

No, no; he must compose himself, have faith, and mourn for Angelo. He must believe that some would survive. He must believe that Angelo had had a little time to meditate on his words before he died. He must talk to the people gathered around him.

After these minutes of silence, which seemed endless, he did talk. His voice was trembling, and his face was ashen. He addressed himself especially to the neighbors, Signor Ristori and Signora Del Francia, and said, "We have just heard on the radio that a friend of mine was killed in the war. He was a person very dear to me. The sun did not rise this morning for Angelo Luzzatto. But there is nothing we can do except pray." Then, turning to the guests, he said, "We must say Kaddish."

"But," said Ernesto, "there are not ten males here."

"It is true," Pardo acknowledged. He was so upset that he had overlooked the fact that to say Kaddish, the traditional prayer for the dead, ten Jewish men have to be present according to the orthodox Jewish rite. This habit of not permitting certain prayers or religious services to take place if fewer than ten male Jews were present apparently was established long ago to prevent an extreme

8. Isaiah 11:6.
9. Ezekiel 6:8.

scattering of Jewish people and to promote the existence of small communities of at least ten families, each man representing one family.

"The circumstances do not permit us to say Kaddish," added Pardo. "We must say a different prayer."

Mr. Ristori, one of the neighbors who had come for water, said in a hesitant voice, "Signor Pardo, five of us who are here are not Jews. We are Christians, but we share your sorrow. Can we stay here with you, during your prayers?"

"Certainly," replied Pardo, and he, Dario, Teofilo, Cesare, and Ernesto looked for yarmulkas and hats to put on. Pardo started to pray. It was a prayer in Hebrew, and with the exception of Pardo nobody could fully understand its meaning. Pardo recited it with a sad, slow, firm, and deep voice. Everyone was listening, everyone was partaking. The five Christians in particular were listening intensely to the sound, making a strong effort to penetrate the obscure meaning. Everyone was pervaded by the devotion, the sorrow, the piety, the faith of the moment.

Pardo had recited almost two-thirds of the prayer when voices were heard from the street. Then there was a loud knocking at the street door of the house. Everybody looked at one another; everybody understood. This was the knock that in some inaccessible part of their souls the seven Jews had been waiting for, the knock of death. Nobody moved. Pardo continued the prayer with a firm and grief-stricken voice.

The Confrontation

The knocking grew louder and then was followed by the sound of boots and rifle butts battering the door. Finally there was a crash. The door had been broken in, and through it came a squad of German soldiers fully armed and in uniform. The motor of an armored truck parked in front of the house had been left running. About twenty soldiers came in, led by an older man who seemed to be an officer of some sort. "Nobody move," he said in Italian with a strong German accent. "Whoever moves will be shot immediately." Then in German he ordered some of the soldiers to close all the windows with the double shutters common in Italian houses, and to close the double shutters of the doors to the garden, so that no light could come in from outside. Under no condition could the windows or the shutters be open. Nobody from the street should be able to snipe or to see what was happening inside.

A soldier holding a powerful flashlight and accompanied by two others went through the house carrying out this order. The flashlight hurt everyone's eyes. Pardo, his guests, Silvia, Alice, Giovanna, and the two neighbors were all in the living room not knowing what was going to happen, although by now the Jews in the group felt that they had been trapped and were in a most precarious situation. Some of them believed they were going to be deported. All of them remained mute, watching the Germans, not daring to look at one another.

"Nobody move," repeated the officer in guttural Italian. For expeditions of this type the German army used to select someone who knew a little more than a smattering of the language. "Only you, come here," he said to Pardo. "We know who you are, the rich Jew who hates dogs. The Führer loves dogs and hates Jews." He laughed scornfully, then added, "Because you are so rich, you are still alive today, and nobody has reported you yet. We know very well that you are hiding gold, silver, and diamonds in this house. We will give you a few seconds to find your treasure."

"There is no gold, silver, or diamonds here," murmured Pardo.

"You must find the treasure, Jew," said the officer, grabbing Pardo by his shoulders and gesturing as if to choke him. "Show these soldiers where it is." Two soldiers grabbed the elderly parnas by each arm and a third one started to kick his buttocks and hit him with the stock of a rifle. Pardo, bent forward, was driven in that posture from room to room of the big house in search of the treasure, while the rest remained under guard, with a number of rifles and one machine gun pointed at them.

The search was long, methodical, and minute, room after room, closet after closet, drawer after drawer. Nothing was found. The invisible treasure that was there remained invisible to the Nazis. Pardo, having now been beaten up, was brought back to the officer in charge, while the soldiers showed their empty hands.

"Very well," said the officer, very irritated. Then he gave some hurried orders in German, and a few of the soldiers proceeded to remove furniture, take down paintings from the walls, collect objects, porcelain, antique china, linen, tablecloths, silver sets, and lamps and carry them out into the truck.

Dante Ristori had figured out that this was going to be a hold-up and large-scale burglary. He had seven hundred lire (about forty dollars) in his pocket. Since he was in back of the others and his movements could not be seen, he put this money inside his sock, thinking that it would never be found there.

As witnesses who lived in nearby houses later reported, the big truck was filled three times by the Nazis with things taken from Pardo's house. Three times the empty truck came back. The whole burglary lasted almost three hours, while the prisoners remained under guard of the rifles and the machine gun and in the glaring light of the powerful flashlight.

Only one item did the Nazis leave in the house: the big menorah that was in the back of the living room. The candelabrum with its seven branches stood on its stem, alone and prominent in the bare room. Apparently the Nazis thought that Jewish article was without any redeemable cash value.

When despoliation is perpetrated as an act of hate and is politically instigated or sanctioned by the government, it is an attack not only on the property of the victim, but also on his dignity and his very right to exist. That leftover menorah, however, the one article that Pardo valued most, indicated that the attack had not accomplished its full purpose.

When the looting was finished and the circle of soldiers around the prisoners began to tighten, Pardo felt he had to speak. Addressing himself to the officer, he said, "You have taken everything you wanted. Spare what we have left, our lives." The officer looked at him without answering. Pardo thought that the captain had not understood his Italian and repeated loudly, "You have taken everything you wanted. Spare our lives." Still the officer did not answer. At this point Pardo lost his composure and repeated the sentence several times very loudly, and neighbors in nearby houses reported later that they could hear him saying these words. At this point the captain began by turns to grumble and to laugh in a loud, scornful way, without uttering a word. Pardo understood what he meant and got hold of himself.

"Officer," he said daringly, "since this is my home, I feel I must be the one to speak to you. If what you intend to do to us is because we are Jews, you must know that there are among us five who are Christians. Spare them. One is that woman there, my maid, Silvia Bonanni, and her helpers Giovanna and Alice Ulivari. This lady is Emilia Del Francia and this man is Dante Ristori, two neighbors who came here to get water from the well in the garden and have their containers here. These people are Christians and bear Christian names."

The captain replied, "You have spoken enough, dirty Jew. Another Jewish trick to save some of you."

At this point Dante Ristori, too, understood that what was happening was more than a robbery, and he decided to show that he was a Christian. He took out of his wallet a *santino* and showed it to the Germans. *Santini* are small images of saints or of the Holy Family that many devout Italian Catholics carry in their pockets or wallets. The one Ristori carried represented the likeness of Jesus Christ. Nobody seemed to recognize what he was doing. He continued to hold the *santino* in his right hand, as for protection.

"Officer, these five people are Christians," protested Pardo.

"Shut up, lousy Jew," was the answer. "No Aryan would contaminate himself in the home of a Jew, or ask for his water, or join him in prayer. Shut up, treacherous pig. We shall take care of you later. First you will see what is going to happen to your kind." He gave some quick orders in German to the soldiers, who pushed all the prisoners except Pardo into the little pantry between the garden and the kitchen. There all eleven prisoners were kicked and beaten with rifle butts. Some of them screamed; some moaned. Pardo was left in the living room with the captain and one armed soldier. At a signal from the officer, one of the soldiers threw a hand grenade into the pantry, and a single great explosion silenced all the screams and moans. Pardo understood. Now only he was alive; he and the Germans.

"And now to you," said the captain to Pardo, "you who have so keenly disappointed us by hiding your treasure somewhere outside this house. Now before we get rid of you we shall make you do what we want." Then he crossed over to the bruised elderly man and slapped his face. Pardo did not flinch; he held himself up by leaning against the menorah. The captain thundered, "Jew, you must repeat what I say. Say 'Heil Hitler.'"

Pardo replied in Hebrew at the top of his lungs, almost as if he intended to fill the empty rooms, with the words, *"Adonai melech!"*[1] ("The Lord is King.")

The captain slapped him again on both cheeks and said, "Did you understand me? You must speak in German or Italian. Repeat after me word by word: 'Hitler has become the master of Europe.'"

And Pardo again answered with two Hebrew words: *"Adonai malach!"* ("The Lord has reigned.")

The captain, afraid that he was losing face before his squad and livid with anger, said, "Jew, I give you only one more chance. Say that Nazi Germany will reign over the world for a thousand years."

And Pardo, with a very loud voice and in the direction of the dead, as if he wanted them to hear, too, again exclaimed in Hebrew, *"Adonai yimloch le'olam va'ed!"* ("The Lord will rule forever and ever.")

"Aren't you afraid?" asked the officer furiously.

And again Pardo said in Hebrew, *"Lo irah ra', ki Attah 'imadi.'"*[2] ("I will fear no evil, for Thou art with me.")

"Even when you are about to die you continue to insult the Reich. A Jew to the end. But your end will not be easy. We shall beat you, we shall torture you, blind you, and finally kill you. I'll ask you again, Jew; aren't you afraid?"

"Afraid?" asked Pardo, as if that were an incredible question.

"Yes, afraid," repeated the Nazi, incredulously.

Pardo did not know what to say because, unbelievably, he was not afraid, no longer afraid after a lifetime of possession by fear. The direct confrontation with the carriers of evil had dissolved

1. All Hebrew words are transcribed according to the Sephardic pronunciation.
2. From Psalm 23.

all fear. He was no longer afraid, for God was with him, and as the end was approaching, God was about to reveal to him the secret of his past fears.

The Nazi paused for a few seconds, waiting for an answer, and since he did not get one, said, "We are about to kill you, Jew. Think hard with the last thoughts of which you are still capable; think hard about everybody you can, and tell me: Can you think of anyone who, at this very moment, is worse off than you?"

"Yes," said Pardo at once. *"You."*

The Nazi was taken aback by the effrontery. This Jew, beaten up, about to be tortured, about to die, speaks so to his German captor? Perhaps the Jew meant that Germany was going to be defeated and that a fate worse than that which had befallen the Jews was awaiting the German people. Interpreting Pardo in this way —indeed, believing himself that such a thing might really happen—the officer was seized by a spell of uncontrollable fury. With the metal part of a rifle he hit Pardo in one eye and then in the other; then he beat him again with the stock of the rifle. Pardo, bleeding from his eyes, unable to see, and staggering, still sustained himself with one hand on the stem of the menorah. The officer was intrigued by the Jew's stubbornness, also savoring the suffering he was inflicting and the dialogue of death. He said, "And now, before I finish you off, Jew, let me ask you again. Who is worse off than you?"

"You."

"I suppose you still think of yourself as one of the chosen."

"Chosen to serve God in my way."

"Then you *do* consider yourself chosen?"

"Chosen to bear the brunt of your evil and to denounce it in His name."

"You are about to die and you know it, dog-hater. We are kind to you. Because of us you will not worry any more about dogs or other animals. You will never see them again. You are blind."

"I see, as never before," said Pardo, in an astonishingly loud voice, as if he had regained all his strength and more. "I see all of you around me. I am encircled not by men, but by animals. *You are what I feared throughout my life*, and what now I can finally face, you who have accepted evil and become the bearers of evil and evil itself. You no longer wear the image of God. You have become wolves. You are the animals of my fears. Now I know! I know! I know! No fellow men around me I see." Pardo must have pronounced these words several times and loudly, because neighbors later reported having heard him saying, "You are the animals of my fears, animals, animals."

While the wounded parnas was talking, all the Nazis, officer and men, had stopped beating him, not so much in order to prolong the perverted joy of witnessing his encounter with death, but in order to hear and perhaps understand his strange words. Nazis had the habit of labeling Jews whom they had captured with names of animals, such as pigs, dogs, and rats; and now there was a dying Jew addressing them in the same way. And they understood him when, making an effort to overcome the pain and to muster the strength to speak, he continued in a clear voice, "*You are animals*. Your voice is the barking of hounds, the howling of wolves. In each of you I see a snout, fur, four claws, and a tail." And he repeated "Animals with a snout, fur, four claws, and a tail." And he repeated the same sentence again and again with an unfaltering voice, as if that hypnotic effect that someone in the past had attributed to him were now set free.

But what was to be hypnotic for others was for him the stupendous unveiling of his life secret. Yes, God was with him. By making the Nazis appear as animals, God was revealing that his past fears were indeed the fear of human evil, of which the Nazis were the most perfect representatives in all of human history, the evil that he had always fought off with his friendship and love. Now he no longer feared. Now he knew. He was happy to be alive, even if for only a few more seconds. God was with him, his great partner in the great unveiling.

"Let's finish him off," said the officer. With several soldiers he moved toward him and they resumed their beating with rifles and other implements. The soldier who was still holding the flashlight as he took part in the beating made a wrong move and fell, breaking the flashlight. Now the room was completely dark, and in the dark the Nazis could still hear the weakened voice of the man repeating, "A snout, fur, four claws, and a tail." The words of the moribund had acquired a rhythmic cadence; the weaker his voice, the stronger was the effect, as incantation, curse, hypnotic command. "A snout, fur, four claws, and a tail," they heard once more; then they heard the dying man say more strange Hebrew words, his last: *"Shemah Israel, Adonai Elohenu, Adonai Ehad."*[3] Then silence. The Jew was dead.

Petrified and spellbound, the Nazis felt imprisoned by the darkness of the room. With the death of the Jew the darkness had become more intense. It would have been easy enough to open the shutters of the door to the garden in order to have light again, but nobody made a move to do it, perhaps because they remembered the instructions of the officer that the shutters should not be open under any circumstances; perhaps because they did not want to see whether they had really changed into animals; perhaps because the darkness in the middle of the day reflected the night that they felt inside, in their souls. There was a feeling of total immersion in nothingness. But it did not last long, because the black souls started to feel again.

Was there really silence? None of the soldiers was speaking, and the Jew was dead, yet his words reverberated loudly in their minds: "You are animals . . . a snout, fur, four claws, and a tail."

After an interval of a minute or two, a wave of restlessness and agitation assailed them. Some felt the urge to howl, so strong had

3. The first words of the most common Hebrew prayer, affirming the unity and universality of God. Religious Jews repeat these words when they feel they are about to die.

been the spell of the dying Jew. Could what he said be true? Yes, it was true, some of them felt. Among them were three or four recent draftees, young soldiers with boyish faces, with hands already cruel but hearts not yet completely hardened by the atrocities of the war. They began to touch their own bodies, checking to see whether they had grown fur or a tail and whether their faces had become snouts, and under the power of the suggestion, some of them felt they had indeed changed. But they could not tell. The oppressive, pitch-black obscurity wrapped and entrapped them.

One of them finally remembered that he had a small kerosene lamp to be used in an emergency, and he lit it. The tremulous little flame lit the room somewhat, and they could see the body of the man lying on the floor in a lake of blood. Then the Nazis looked at one another's faces, and yes, they looked different, distorted, horrified. Indeed, they seemed to have acquired animal-like features. Yes, the Jew who had pronounced those strange words in the moment of death had cast a spell on them; he had bewitched them. Some of the youngest started to scream. One of them shouted, "The old man has practiced sorcery on us." Another one added, "We heard in the south of Italy that some people can change men into animals in this country."

The officer said strongly, but with less conviction than usual, "Quiet. Black magic does not make people animals. They thought so in the Dark Ages."

And one of the youngest soldiers replied, "No age was darker than this." Another one said, "That man was a hypnotist. Now he is dead and cannot release us from his hypnotic power." Somebody else murmured, "We have been hypnotized for a long time to be like animals."

The youngest of all had the impression that he saw animals all around, and with an imploring voice he asked, "Comrades in arms, do you see features that you could call human?"

The second youngest replied, "Only on the body of the Jew."

And the youngest asked again with an even more anguished, childlike voice, "Comrades, do you see any man here?"

"One, but he is dead," replied the third youngest.

The very youngest then started to sob and said, "Mother, Mother, will you recognize me?"

At the mention of mother three or four felt tears in their eyes. In the meantime, the kerosene lamp was becoming dimmer and dimmer because the fuel was almost exhausted, and the darkness threatened to entrap them again in the middle of the day. One of the soldiers, pointing to the menorah on which seven candles were still placed, said, "Let's use it!" And with the dim kerosene lamp he lit the seven branches one by one. Now there was light again. The light of the menorah caressed Pardo in the sleep of his death.

"Comrades," said the officer, "do not open the windows. Nobody must see inside. The light of this lamp will help us get out of here."

"And feel like men again," added one of the youngest.

The officer continued. "Those who want to celebrate this expedition can make it into the cellar in spite of the dark. One of you told me there is a case of champagne there."

Most of them went into the cellar, lighted some matches, opened the case of champagne, and drank and drank, and sang and sang obscene German songs. But the three or four youngest ones were helped by the light of the menorah to find their way out. They went directly to the truck and waited for the others.

Almost all those who participated in this expedition were young, and perhaps, when this story is written, some or most, or even all of them are still living, unmolested, somewhere in Germany. Whether any of them is like an olive, retained on the old tree of redemption after the hurricane of evil, and retains a glimmer of the menorah, we human beings do not know. But this we know, that the seven lights that caressed the body of the parnas of Pisa still shine for both the reader and the writer of these pages.

While most of the Germans were drinking and singing, the booming of cannon was heard again. The artillery of the Allies had resumed their work from south of the Arno, a few yards away, as if a winged messenger had crossed the river and informed them of the event in Sant' Andrea Street and as if they were protesting and reaffirming that the fight for freedom might at times slow up but never cease. The Nazis quickly regrouped, put a sign on the door of the house, "Achtung. House Mined," and left in the truck, most of them screaming and singing, drunk with alcohol and blood.

In Sant' Andrea Street

When the people who lived in Sant' Andrea Street heard the German truck leave, they did not go out to see what had happened. Even when the cannons of the Allies stopped their new barrage, they did not move. Because of the curfew, they couldn't go outside except between 10 A.M. and 12 noon. Thus they would have to wait until the following day to get near Pardo's house. They knew also that the Germans would not like the idea of their investigating and had probably put up a warning not to enter the place.

Fear, however, did not immobilize all of them. Two responded to the urging of their hearts, a Christian and a Jew. The Christian was Umberto Pecori, a cabinetmaker and restorer of antique furniture. He had seen his brother-in-law Dante Ristori (husband of his wife's sister) enter Pardo's home to get water, and he was extremely concerned.

The other was Manlio Lascar, a poor Jew who had remained rather remote from the Jewish community because he had married a Christian against his family's wishes. When he heard the noise coming from Pardo's house, Manlio Lascar, who was hidden in another house in Sant' Andrea Street, felt himself very much a Jew and urgently wanted to find out what had happened and whether he could be of any help.

Pecori and Lascar, making as little noise as possible and without being seen by anybody, went independently to Pardo's house. They met there. What they saw made them cry, but they did not lose control of themselves. They had only one aim: to see whether anyone was still alive. And indeed, they did find two people who appeared to be dead but were actually alive. One was Dante Ristori, still holding the image of Jesus Christ in his right hand. The other was Dario Gallichi, stained all over with blood, maimed, missing a leg, but still breathing. Pecori and Lascar decided to put the two wounded men on a cart standing nearby, and by hand they pushed the cart to the hospital. This was not an unusual scene. Apparently the authorities allowed people to take wounded persons to the hospital in spite of the curfew.

Dario Gallichi was still alive when he reached the hospital. He was too sick to be treated and died within a few minutes. But at least he had returned to his hospital—did he know it?—the place to which he had dreamed one day of going back, the place where, he had said, he wanted to die.

Dante Ristori, too, was about to die. Pecori knew that his niece Elvira, Dante's daughter, had found refuge from the bombing in the palace of the archbishop, near the square of the leaning tower, just two blocks away from the hospital. He sent for her. As Elvira Ristori later told me, her father was still alive when she arrived, but he expired shortly afterwards, still holding in his right hand the image of Jesus Christ with which he had tried to protect himself. Elvira Ristori undressed her father, and when she took off one of his socks, she found the seven hundred lire that he had put there. They were saved for her. Elvira Ristori is in her eighties now, and she still mourns for her father with tears in her eyes, still full of indignation at the event, and full of sweet memories of Pardo, his fiacre, and especially his Fridays, when she and her family could have a meal because of him.

But nobody in Sant' Andrea Street knew what Manlio Lascar and Umberto Pecori had done. The following day at ten o'clock, when people were allowed to leave their homes, a group of neighbors gathered in front of Pardo's house to find out what had happened. They reviewed with one another the terrible things they had heard: the breaking of the door, the beating, the screaming, the grenade, and the loud voice of Pardo. Now the house was quiet. Could anybody go inside? The Germans had put up a sign: "Achtung (attention). House Mined," yet somebody might still be alive and could be saved. The silence was ominous, though. The people gathered in Sant' Andrea Street knew that yesterday's expedition had been a German attack against Jews, and they could not understand. Why? Signor Pardo had always been so good, so generous, so helpful to everybody. Who would have told the Nazis where he lived? And yet somebody must have informed on him. The people gathered there concluded that no Christian who lived in Sant' Andrea Street and knew Pardo would ever have told the Nazis where he lived. But one in the crowd said—and others agreed—"I was looking out my window when I saw the German officer talking to Enrico Giordano. The German asked him where Israel's big capitalist lived, and Giordano indicated the place."

"Enrico Giordano? Why would he do that?"

"Obviously he did not know what the Germans were about," said one.

"But I heard Margherita Palagini, who lives one floor below him, say to Giordano from the stairs, 'Don't tell the Germans where he lives,'" said a neighbor.

"Giordano just became a member of the Republican Fascist Party," somebody murmured.

"Giordano recently got into a dispute about the garden. Signor Pardo was the landlord, and he thought Palagini was entitled to the garden," said a neighbor.

"No, it cannot be," said another of Pardo's neighbors, shaking his head.

Giovanni Palagini was there and said, "I, too, was about to go to Signor Pardo's home to get water, but I saw the Germans, and I stopped."

All of a sudden a scream came from the crowd. The one who screamed was a relative of Emilia Del Francia. "Emilia! Emilia!" People then realized that not only Jews, but Christians, too, were in the house. Why had they not come out? What to do now? While the indecision persisted and the anguish increased, some people thought of informing the monks and priests in the nearby cloister and church of San Francesco, about a hundred yards away. Maybe they would do something about it.

The friars, who the previous day had heard the shouting and screaming, agreed to come and help. Father Bonaventura, with some young friars, arrived on the scene. The crowd withdrew to let the group of monks and priests enter for the first time into the house of a Jew. The churchmen could not help making sounds of horror and dismay when they saw the bodies in the pantry, some of them badly dismembered. They carefully examined them one by one to see whether anyone was still alive and could receive medical attention. Everyone was dead. The friars came back to the front of the house and crossed themselves. Everybody understood. The crowd burst into a scream of horror and dismay.

A person in the crowd then announced, "I have just heard that somebody took to the hospital two persons who were in Signor Pardo's house, and they too died."

The old priest asked some neighbors to identify the bodies. Pardo was easily identified, still lying in front of the menorah. When the body of Silvia Bonanni, the maid, was recognized, it was put close to Pardo's body. Somebody went into the garden, cut two branches from a small tree, and made a cross, which was put at Silvia's head. Somebody else put a lighted candlestick on each side of her. Some persons noticed that the Jewish candelabrum had only the remains of the candles, probably melted down during the night. They went to their homes to look for new candles—hard to find in those days when electricity was so scarce —and came back with seven of them, which they lighted. Now the menorah and the cross were next to each other, and the light of the seven branches merged with that of the candlesticks. And the men and women who were gathered there seemed to understand that when a light enlightens people, it can be only one light.

The old priest then gave instructions to the young friars. "Brothers," he said, "we must take care of the bodies. We shall keep them in the courtyard of the cloister until they can be buried. We must be sure of the identifications and then separate them into two groups. We shall take the bodies of the Christians to our chapel and then to our cemetery. We shall see that the bodies of the Jews are sent to the Jewish cemetery."

At this point a young friar could not check his agitation and said, "Father, I do not understand. I do not understand. These people met God and the Supreme Truth together, and you want to separate them again!"

"Brother," the old priest replied calmly, "bodies belong to this world and are treated according to the ways of the world. But don't be concerned. Wherever these people are, they are together, and together they will remain in the memory of those who come to know their story."

Conclusion

The Americans crossed the Arno River in Pisa on September 2, 1944. Mussolini was executed by the partisans on April 28, 1945. Hitler committed suicide on April 30, 1945. Germany surrendered unconditionally on May 7, 1945.

After the end of the war, Dr. Naftoli Emdin, a member of the Jewish congregation of Pisa, brought charges against Enrico Giordano for disclosing to the Germans the address of Giuseppe Pardo Roques. Giordano was arrested, and the trial took place in Florence on March 27, 1946. He was defended by lawyers Gino Gattai and Sirio Saggini. Attorney Eugenio Massart represented Lucia Gallichi, daughter of two victims, Teofilo and Ida Gallichi, and sister of a third, Cesare Gallichi.

Francesco Malerbi reported that he saw Enrico Giordano speaking to the German officer. The following people reported that they had heard the loud, anguished voice of Pardo Roques during the tragic event: Gabriele Macarti, Ireneo Ispani, Velia Serra, Emilio Tedeschi, Mario Rossi, Gina Coscia, Faustino Frangini, Ugo Ario, Gino Lascar, and Angelo Petrini. Father Bonaventura testified about the collection and disposition of the bodies.

Enrico Giordano admitted that he had belonged to the Republican Fascist Party, and that there had been an argument about the garden. He also admitted that when the Nazi officer asked him where "Israel's big capitalist" lived, he gave the information, but he stated that he had no inkling whatsoever that the Nazis "would commit such nefarious action against such a nice man." After fifteen minutes' deliberation, the court concluded that Giordano's intent to hurt could not be proved. He was absolved for insufficient evidence and immediately released from prison. According to Italian law only the public prosecutor (*Procuratore della Republica*) could have appealed the sentence, but he did not.

Approximately eight months earlier, in a public ceremony on August 1, 1945, the first anniversary of the massacre, the city of Pisa had put a memorial plaque on the façade of the home of Giuseppe Pardo Roques. The text of the plaque and an English translation are on pages 146–147.

Epilogue

My story ended with the conclusion. And yet, probably because I am a psychiatrist, I feel impelled to add this epilogue.

The reader remembers that when I left Italy and went to visit Pardo for the last time, he told me that perhaps one day, if I returned, I might help him. I really hoped I would eventually be able to do so. On account of his age and the seriousness of his illness, my grandiose aim to help him psychiatrically could not have been realized to any very significant degree even if I had seen him again. At any rate, the possibility of trying was not given to me. What was given to me, however, was to help others with the same illness, and to make an attempt to understand his case, so that the words put into his mouth in this book would coincide with what I understood.

Pardo did encourage my studies in psychiatry. He introduced me to Professor Enzo Bonaventura, who at that time was one of the few scholars in Italy interested in psychoanalysis. Born in Pisa, the professor then lived in Florence. Later he emigrated to Israel, and in 1948 he was killed there in an Arab ambush.

Bonaventura wrote a book on psychoanalysis, one of the best on the subject in the Italian language, and one of the first psychoanalytic books I read. Bonaventura gave a copy of this book to

Pardo with a personal inscription. I borrowed it, and when I left for America in a great hurry, I inadvertently put that book with the few others I took with me. Shortly after my arrival in New York, a few months before the beginning of World War II, I wrote to Signor Pardo informing him that I had taken the book by mistake and asking him if I could keep it. He promptly replied with a friendly letter in which, among other things, he politely told me that he could not give me the book as a present because it had been personally inscribed to him by the author. I could keep the book for now, but when I visited him again, I would have to return it. The book is still with me, a precious memento of two people I admired. The book did not help me to understand phobias, but it did open up a greater understanding of the human psyche.

In chapter four we found Pardo willing to speak about the last part of his childhood and the beginning of his adolescence. What he is reported to have said reflects what I have come to know about many phobic patients. I have found that the phobic symptom very seldom has anything to do with sexual wishes buried in the unconscious. Although a single striking episode occasionally precipitates the illness, as a rule a general climate of anxiety is necessary. In my experience the climate of anxiety quite often is related to disturbed family relations in childhood. In some cases the social environment plays a dominant or an additional role. Some particularly sensitive and gifted children and adolescents —a few of whom had a normal early childhood that was permeated by basic optimism about people, life, and the promise of the future—become badly disappointed later, at times as early as middle or late childhood, at other times in adolescence or young adulthood. From a state of optimistic innocence they brusquely pass to what they consider constant exposure to the mysterious unpredictability of life, to the sneak attack of danger, or to the errors and malevolence of others. People, life, and the future become suffused with danger. They must be careful. The danger is intangible, and it seems immense and omnipresent because it may manifest itself unpredictably at any moment. This interpretation is not an application of Jean-Jacques Rousseau's concept that man is born innocent and society makes him bad. The state of innocence may also come from a pristine and partial understanding of the environment. Having shaped the world in accordance with the image of a love received unconditionally from his mother, the child or adolescent is, as I said, badly disappointed later, for a number of reasons that may vary in each individual case. At times what the youngster reads in history, literature, or current newspapers or learns in school gradually dissolves his pristine naïveté.

When the sensitive youngster has made these unpleasant realizations and continues to feel terribly disappointed, he has difficulties in facing life. How can he trust, how can he love or retain a loving attitude towards fellow human beings? He might then become suspicious and paranoid; he might become a detached person unable to love. But this is not the case with the phobic. The phobic is a person who retains his ability to love. As a matter of fact, in my long psychiatric career I have never seen a phobic person who was not a loving person. I have made this observation repeatedly, starting with the very first patient I ever treated, Pietro. Does the reader remember him? He was a loving father and husband. He also showed love to me—his improvised first psychotherapist—when, after completing medical school, I prepared to escape from Italy. Against governmental recommendations, Pietro gave me the names of his relatives in London who helped me on my arrival there, one of the stops on my way to America. And during the war, when the illness confined him to the block where he resided, he helped people caught in the ruins and saved lives. As we saw, he did not act this way in order to be recognized as a hero; he was actualizing his love for his neighbor in a way that his illness permitted and facilitated.

The phobic patient can retain the capacity to love and to maintain even intense contacts with life because his anxiety, or sensitivity to danger, becomes displaced and confined to particular situations, things, or animals (they may be bridges, squares, dogs, horses, and so on). The rest of the world continues to be accepted by the patient and may still arouse love in him.

Concerning Giuseppe Pardo Roques, I can advance only hypotheses supported by the cases of phobias that I have studied. There was no doubt that he retained a great deal of love for his fellow man. Possibly when, as an adolescent, he reappraised life in a disappointing way, by means of the unconscious mechanisms described by Freud, he shifted his concern about danger from fellow human beings to animals. For a sensitive person like him, it was impossible to accept the ancient dictum that man is a wolf to other men. He had to transform it into *Lupus homini lupus* ("Only a wolf acts like a wolf to man"). Little Hans, described by Freud, did the same. He changed "Father is a horse to Hans" into "Only a horse is a horse to Hans." In all these cases an effort is made to see the source of the unpredictable risk not in the human, but in the nonhuman. In all the cases that have come to my attention, an unconscious effort was made by the psyche of the patient to respect human dignity and to preserve a disposition to love humans. Thus it seems to me that it is possible to recognize in the illness, too, what can be called a spiritual quality that is a way not only of defending oneself, but also of protecting the human image and humankind.

Unless the patient is treated psychoanalytically, he is almost always unaware of the symbolic meanings and the unconscious motivations of his symptoms. He generally accepts them literally or at their face value. Only rarely, when the patient is confronted with a very intense or even heroic situation, can his awareness overcome the barrier of the unconscious to grasp the meaning of his phobia.

In my version of the events, that is what happened to Giuseppe Pardo Roques in the last moments of his life. When the neighbors heard him saying to the Germans, "You are the animals, animals," it seems to me that he must have referred to the animals of his phobias. The tragic intensity of those last moments presented his mind with the capacity for creating images that usually only dreams and the visions of the mentally ill have. The evildoers whom he faced with blind eyes assumed animal forms; thus he understood that the animals he had been afraid of stood for the men who bring horror and terror to the world. The Nazis, the typical vehicles of evil, appeared as wolves or other animals.

The secret of his illness was thus disclosed. The truth, hidden in the queer features of his infirmity, was finally unveiled by a confrontation with what that truth referred to—the force of evil. That momentary epiphanic vision, which could last no longer than his last instants on earth, was lived by him as a permanent truth and revealed that his illness was an inherent and genuine part of him, bespeaking the truth of his life.

If we apply to the episode a psychiatric terminology, we can say that under the stress of that tragic moment Pardo's phobic condition changed into lycanthropy. Some of the German soldiers, too, may have experienced other phenomena of lycanthropy. Lycanthropy is a mental condition characterized by the belief that a person or persons have become transformed into animals. People allegedly changed into animals may be persons who surrounded the individual who has this belief, members of the group to which he belongs, or the person himself. Although the word is generally used to indicate a delusion of transformation into any animal, in its etymological origin from Greek the term means that a human being has become a wolf. The ancient dictum *Homo homini lupus* becomes actualized in the abnormal imagination.

Myths of various people have described the transformations of human beings into animals. Nebuchadnezzar, king of Babylon, thought that he had become a wolf, and St. Patrick is reported to have transformed Veneticus, king of Gallia, into a wolf. Transformations into animals have not infrequently been portrayed in literature also. One can think of *Steppenwolf* by Hesse, *Metamorphosis* by Kafka, and *Rhinoceros* by Ionesco.

In modern psychiatry the term *lycanthropy* is used most of the time to designate the delusion of an individual schizophrenic patient of having become a wolf or another animal, or of seeing that transformation taking place in other people. This delusion is relatively rare, and some psychiatrists (especially those who do not treat many schizophrenic patients) have never seen a case. I have seen several cases of individual lycanthropy. It is always an extremely disturbing experience. One patient, while attending medical school against his own wishes and in order to comply with those of his parents, one day saw a professor and his assistant gradually becoming horses. They rapidly assumed equine form, and the patient felt unable to stop the phenomenon. Another patient of mine, a phobic with schizophrenic tendencies, thought she had become a dog. This belief lasted three days.

The delusion of being transformed into a wolf is the most common form of lycanthropy. A patient of mine, a loving and warm person, while in a hotel room in a big city during a business trip, started to think about his pretty wife, who had caused him much pain and humiliated him in a thousand ways. All of a sudden, and against his will, he developed the urge to hurt her physically; and while he was experiencing that urge, he realized he had become a wolf. It was a devastating, all-engrossing experience, horrifying beyond description. He did not feel that he was like a wolf, but that he *was* a wolf. What if people saw him in that state; what if somebody knocked at the door? What if somebody called him on the phone, and he answered with a howl? And what if his mother were the person who called? This was the most horrifying of the possibilities, that his mother would find out he had become a wolf. He found himself crying, "Mother, Mother, will you recognize me?" The psychotic episode of my patient was of short duration. In all cases that I have seen, this symptom was lived as an unshakeable reality, was extremely painful, and was never recognized by the patient in its metaphorical meaning until recovery occurred.

Lycanthropy, however, is not always an indication of schizophrenia. In the Middle Ages many cases of it developed in Europe in the form of "collective psychosis." Groups of people, generally belonging to fanatic religious sects, became convinced that they had been transformed into animals. Some cases of lycanthropy occur even now in some mountain villages of Italy. A psychiatric study of lycanthropy by Dr. Jules Bemporad and me has been reported in the medical literature.

When lycanthropy occurs in groups, it generally results from some kind of collective hysteria. A feeling of guilt and unworthiness, so strong as to make the persons believe they do not deserve to belong to the human race, seems to be the underlying cause of this condition. A cultural environment predisposed to beliefs of this kind is necessary. The belief in one's metamorphosis into animal form would not be accepted with absolute certainty unless a group of peers (acting like a collective conscience) shared the same conviction.

In some other situations lycanthropy is a hypnotic phenomenon and is not necessarily related to mental illness. A person who believes he sees people changing into animals is a leader of some special cults, like the Macumba of Brazil, or an individual with hypnotic power who gives a command. The command is experienced immediately as actualizing itself; that is, the transformation takes place right away. The leader may be on the side of the group or against the group. He is a person endowed with mystical power or some extraordinary force that cannot be controlled. For the effect to take place there must be the conviction on the part of the persons involved that they deserve to be the object of such an injunction. According to my version of the events, it was not difficult for some of the young soldiers who participated in the massacre to experience this uncanny force in a person like Giuseppe Pardo Roques, whom many people considered endowed with a strange type of hypnotic power. The majesty of Pardo's confrontation with their crime, the reemergence of human guilt in spite of Nazi indoctrination, and the darkness of the room provided the setting for the astounding experience.

In my version of the story, the few young Germans who were possessed by Pardo's spell and saw themselves changed into animals reached a pivotal point in their lives and had a chance to retrieve their human spirituality. But what about the others who had not felt the horror and the benefit of the spell? Where are they? Will they allow their searching souls to go back to the morning of August 1, 1944, in Pisa, in Sant' Andrea Street?

These last questions indicate that knowledge of Pardo's illness must be placed in the greater context of the healthy part of him; and even more, it must be placed in the huge context of the most serious illness that has afflicted mankind, a moral illness that seems beyond human understanding. Those who want to forget, to hide, or not to have their peace disturbed by what seems inconceivable must face the fact that the inconceivable was conceived and largely implemented. Society at large has not yet acquired sufficient knowledge of the Holocaust, and twentieth-century culture has not yet absorbed its whole meaning. The destiny of mankind may to a large extent depend on the understanding that future generations have of the Holocaust and on the way they respond to this new awareness of the full potentiality of evil. If oblivion or undue permissiveness are allowed to hide the knowledge that what was called the Final Solution was to a considerable extent accomplished, man may move toward another and greater and realistically possible Final Solution for which there will be no chosen people, but for which all people will be chosen. Will this be man's last choice?

No, Giuseppe Pardo Roques would say. For if awareness of the full potentiality of evil is acquired, mankind will not allow a similar event ever again to darken the earth. The greater the evil, the greater must be the understanding and the love required to undo that evil. Precursors of this greater understanding and of this greater love are at times hidden in obscure ideas and in strange forms of suffering and pain. They might be found in mental illness.

Acknowledgments

I wish to thank the following persons who helped me collect the information necessary for writing this book.

Attorney Guido De Cori, president of the Jewish congregation of Pisa.

Dr. Giulio Arieti, my brother, who helped me to trace a number of witnesses.

Mrs. Elvira Ristori Bindi, daughter of the victim Dante Ristori and niece of Umberto Pecori.

Mrs. Marisa Perdon, daughter of Manlio Lascar.

Giovanni Palagini, tenant and neighbor of Giuseppe Pardo Roques.

Luciana Tinucci, neighbor of Giuseppe Pardo Roques.

The newspaper *Il Tirreno* of Leghorn, for providing photocopies of the articles covering the trial of Enrico Giordano.

Professor Giorgio Del Guerra and Dr. Lilia Paradisi d'Elia, director of the library of the University of Pisa, for offering evidence of the authenticity of the story of Abramo Pace, reported in chapter two. (The original source was the writing of the Pisan historian Pio Pecchiai.)

Mr. Sergio Dello Strogolo, for preparing some of the maps and pictures.

I wish to thank also Mrs. Joann Kirtland, my secretary and editor, and my son Dr. James Arieti for numerous valuable suggestions.

My gratitude goes to Mrs. Midge Decter for her deep involvement with this book and for her generously given advice.

ACCOLTI A FRATERNA DIFESA
IN QUESTA CASA OSPITALE DI
GIUSEPPE PARDO ROQUES
CITTADINO STIMATO E IN TEMPI NON TRISTI
PRO SINDACO DI PISA
IL 1 AGOSTO DEL 1944
EBBERO INSIEME MORTE

PARDO ROQUES GIUSEPPE
GALLICHI PROF. DARIO
GALLICHI TEOFILO
DE CORI IDA NEI GALLICHI
GALLICHI CESARE
LEVI DOTT. ERNESTO
LEVI CESIRA NEI LEVI
EBREI
ULIVARI GIOVANNA
ULIVARI ALICE
BONANNI SILVIA
DEL FRANCIA EMILIA
RISTORI DANTE
CRISTIANI

CHE IL CRIMINALE ODIO DI RAZZA
E LA SANGUINARIA FURIA NAZISTA
ACCOMUNARONO NEL TRAGICO DESTINO
E NELLA PIETA MEMORE DEGLI UOMINI

NEL PRIMO ANNIVERSARIO
DELLA STRAGE ESECRANDA
IL COMUNE DI PISA QUESTO MARMO PONE
RICORD, MONITO, AUSPICIO DI UMANA FRATERNITA

WHILE IN BROTHERLY DEFENSE
THEY WERE GATHERED TOGETHER
IN THIS HOSPITABLE HOME OF
GIUSEPPE PARDO ROQUES
ESTEEMED CITIZEN AND
VICEMAYOR OF PISA
IN A PERIOD OF TIME
WHICH WAS NOT SORROWFUL
ON 1 AUGUST 1944
TOGETHER MET DEATH

GIUSEPPE PARDO ROQUES
PROFESSOR DARIO GALLICHI
TEOFILO GALLICHI
IDA GALLICHI, BORN DE CORI
CESARE GALLICHI
DOCTOR ERNESTO LEVI
CESIRA LEVI, BORN LEVI
JEWS
GIOVANNA ULIVARI
ALICE ULIVARI
SILVIA BONANNI
EMILIA DEL FRANCIA
DANTE RISTORI
CHRISTIANS

THE CRIMINAL RACIAL HATRED
AND THE BLOODTHIRSTY NAZI FURY
UNITED THEM IN TRAGIC DESTINY
AND IN THE COMPASSIONATE MEMORY OF MEN

ON THE FIRST ANNIVERSARY
OF THE INFAMOUS MASSACRE
THE CITY OF PISA PLACES THIS MARBLE
AS A REMEMBRANCE, A WARNING AND
AN AUSPICE OF HUMAN BROTHERHOOD